Corporate Cruise Murder

Dawn Brookes

Corporate Cruise Murder

A Rachel Prince Mystery

Dawn Brookes

Dawn Brookes
Publishing

Oakwood Publishing

Paperback Edition 2022
Kindle Edition 2022
Paperback ISBN: 978-1-913065-67-6
Hardback ISBN: 978-1-913065-68-3
Copyright © DAWN BROOKES 2021
Cover Images: AdobeStockImages
Cover Design: John & Janet

In memory of my good friend Linda

Chapter 1

Darrell Baker whistled a tune while heading for the hotel reception desk. He had struggled to get out of bed, which meant packing in a hurry. Now, he intended to enjoy a whole day exploring Mumbai by himself.

He handed his room key over to the same skinny receptionist who'd been on duty when he checked in the evening before. Darrell rarely remembered people he regarded as insignificant, but this guy irritated him. He smiled too much, and he was doing it again. A false grin that didn't reach the eyes was plastered the width of his long, thin face.

"Mr Baker, I hope you enjoyed your stay. Next time, you should try to stay longer."

Did he just wink? Nah, surely not!

He'd got Darrell's attention but wasn't waiting for a reply. The guy held out his long-fingered hand.

Backing off to avoid touching the cream vellum envelope on offer, Darrell barked, "What's that? My bill's being paid for by the company. Check your records." He automatically thrust his hands in his pockets, feeling acid rise to his throat. No way was he paying for a few hours' sleep in a five-star hotel. He wouldn't have emptied the minibar to counter the jet lag if he'd realised he'd be footing the cost.

"Your bill is in order, sir. I was instructed to hand you this letter on checkout. I believe it's a message from your company."

Darrell snatched the envelope, letting out a heavy sigh of relief. It wouldn't surprise him if the annoying bloke had already looked inside. Turning his back on the reception desk, he ripped the envelope open. His jaw dropped when he read the contents.

"Now?" He spun his head back in the receptionist's direction, but the guy had moved on and was already focusing his pasted-on smile towards someone else. Darrell scrunched the note up tight and threw it at a nearby bin. It missed by a couple of inches, but so what? Darrell turned to go.

"You might wanna pick that up." He would have ignored the interference except he recognised the deep baritone Texas accent. This day couldn't get any worse. He spiralled on his heels, eyeing the thrown away note on the floor next to a pair of brown shoes polished to within an inch of their life.

"Erm… oops. I didn't realise I'd missed."

The glowering Earl Spence didn't budge when Darrell bent down to pick up his rubbish. They both knew he didn't believe a word.

"We meet in person at last." The silver-grey haired man with a neatly trimmed moustache was as condescending in person as he was online.

Darrell felt a knot tighten in his stomach, already regretting donning Bermuda shorts and a white vest for his day out. How was he to know he'd be meeting the PR officer face-to-face for the first time? Earl was the man Darrell suspected would have a major, if not final, say on his upcoming promotion. In Darrell's mind, the promotion was a foregone conclusion, but something in Earl's tone sent alarm bells shooting through his head. Surely the man wouldn't hold a small thing like tossing a bit of litter against him?

Time to reset. Straightening up, he held out his hand.

"Wonderful to meet you face-to-face, Mr Spence. What a coincidence running into you. Are you on vacation?"

"Kind of," said the Texan. A tight-lipped grin suggested there were more shocks to follow. Darrell's hand felt sweaty as Earl's penetrating grip released it. His self-assured confidence was diminishing by the second.

"I believe you got our note," Earl said scornfully, staring at the letter in the bin. "You need to wait over there." He inclined his head towards a table upon which a man sporting a white turban was laying tea-trays. Darrell recognised the one person already at the table. Pearl Pantoni was one of the party he was meant to be meeting on board the cruise ship later. They'd only ever met through online meetings.

Trust her to be first. Looking at Earl, Darrell was about to remonstrate and confess that he'd been intending to ignore the note, store his case in the hotel luggage room and go sightseeing. He'd prebooked a tuk-tuk to tour the city.

Earl's cold eyes made him think better of it. This guy had no sense of humour, so best not let on he'd been hoping to avoid the team building until they were aboard the cruise liner. And, even then, he planned to put in the minimum of effort just to play the game.

"Right. I see Pearl's already there," he said, recovering. "Have a pleasant trip, Mr Spence, whatever you're doing."

"I will, boy. I will." Earl's habit of calling people 'boy', or 'sweetheart' if they were women, was barely tolerable online, but here in India? Use of the word and his dismissal implied Darrell was some sort of servant. Darrell had a sneaking suspicion Earl Spence wasn't here on a sightseeing tour, especially as he knew the contents of the blasted letter.

Trying to appear confident, he took his suitcase and strolled over to the table where Pearl was already pouring tea. Darrell clenched his fists when he sat down. An inner rage threatened to consume him, but it was coupled with fear.

Without so much as a hello to the woman, Darrell snapped, "Do you know what he's doing here?"

"Good to meet you, too." She raised a disapproving eyebrow.

"Yeah, cool. But what's *he* doing here?"

"Who?" Pearl added two lumps of brown sugar to her drink.

"Spence," he snapped, suspecting she knew full well who he was referring to. He was being unreasonable, but he didn't have to care about offending her. She was a weakling, and Darrell Baker didn't tolerate weaklings. He had no reason to impress her; she wasn't in the running for his job.

Pearl didn't appear surprised or put out when she looked over to where Earl stood, confirming his hunch. The PR officer was pretending not to watch them. Her tone was resigned when she answered.

"I wouldn't know. Would you like tea or coffee?"

"Coffee." Darrell's eyes were firmly fixed on Earl, who had now turned his back on them. A quiet but firm response jarred his attention.

"It's in the tall pot."

Taken by surprise, he snapped his neck back in Pearl's direction. Darrell had never really looked at Pearl Pantoni before, mainly because she hardly spoke during the meetings, or rather arguments. The latter were all too frequent when the CEO wasn't around. Pantoni was the oldest of the senior research scientists, or SRSs as they were known to each other.

Darrell shrugged and poured himself a black coffee before appraising the woman sitting opposite. She wore a sky-blue business suit, complementing navy-blue eyes that somehow seemed brighter in the airy lobby. He had to admit she wasn't bad looking for a woman who must be fifteen years older than he was. No wedding ring, he noted, shooting her one of his flashiest grins.

"It seems weird, doesn't it? Us not meeting in person before. I feel like we know each other, but don't, if you know what I mean?" *One-nil to me*, he thought as the corners of her lips inched upwards and her cheeks flushed slightly.

"To be honest, I'm worried about meeting everyone. I'll be the oldest here."

"Really? You don't look much older than me," he lied. "But then you do work for Rejuvenescence Pharma." He burst out laughing at his own joke.

Pearl's cheeks flushed a deeper red as she giggled. "Do you think so?"

"Absolutely. And don't be concerned about meeting the others. We're all in the same boat."

"Ship," she corrected.

He laughed again until he realised, from her serious expression, she hadn't been making a joke. "I said boat… you said ship," he tried to explain but drew a blank. "Anyway, it's a pleasure to meet you at last, Dr Pantoni." He offered his hand, and she shook it. "How was London when you left? I was born there, you know."

"I wondered about your accent, and please call me Pearl. You have a sort of American-London twang. It's nice." She flushed again.

"You can take the boy out of London, but you can't take London out of the boy," he said, grinning.

"You're better off where you are. London was freezing cold when I left, but I'm homesick already. I only ever travel abroad for work. This will be my first holiday, if that's what team building is. How was your flight?"

"Loooong, and the jet lag's a pain. I have to say, New York was pretty cold when I left as well. If I'm honest, I was hoping to get a tour of Mumbai today before boarding the ship. Then I got the summons, so here I am. I take it you got one too?" He had already spotted the envelope jutting out of the side pocket of her handbag. "I suppose the others will receive the same thing. It appears team building starts here and now."

"I suspect this trip's going to be full of surprises." Pearl's eyelids dropped towards her cup.

"What makes you say that?" Darrell's heart pounded as more acid attacked his throat.

"Because, in my experience, when a big promotion's up for grabs, the boss and her sidekick are usually very hands-on. The vultures also come out. I don't believe team building is the top priority. It's just a smokescreen to get us to drop our guard. Earl's presence suggests Dr Stone hasn't yet made her mind up. If I were to hazard a guess at why he's here, it would be that she's summoned him to make sure they choose the right person." Her eyes locked on Darrell's. Not gloating, more like telegraphing a message with an air of sympathy.

Darrell's stomach lurched. "Are you suggesting Spence's coming on the cruise?"

"Not just him. If he's here, Dr Stone will also join us. Earl will be here to help her handpick a person who won't give the company a bad name, but take heart: she always makes the final decision."

A smug grin replaced the sympathetic one. The wallflower was turning out to be a thorn bush. At least she had given him a small spark of hope. Tia Stone would choose in the end. He knew she liked him and had already showed her preference. Still, he was clearly in a battle to prove himself now, but was annoyed about the team-building sham. If that's what this was.

"She emailed us all and told us to go away and enjoy ourselves. Why would she do that if she was planning on coming?"

"Maybe she's having second thoughts." The sympathetic eye returned. Darrell was struggling to work Pearl Pantoni out.

"Or it's just a horrible coincidence meeting Spence, and he's taking a holiday in India."

"In his business suit? I doubt that. And I do hope Dr Stone is coming because, if she's sent him on his own, it's going to be a hell of a week."

Darrell's head followed Pearl's gaze. Earl Spence was in conversation with four of the other research scientists. They were meeting face-to-face for the first time. Watching Earl cosying up to Darrell's biggest rival, Carol North, he got a lump in his throat that tightened along with more acid, almost choking him. If only he hadn't drunk the minibar dry.

"I'm looking forward to meeting Carol," said Pearl. "She's had run-ins with Dr Stone a few times. We've got a lot in common."

"Oh, I didn't know that." Darrell relaxed a little, feeling better about his chances again. "What kind of run-ins?"

"She disagreed on SAE reporting in the last trial."

SAEs were serious adverse events, which had to be scrupulously reported to the senior board and recorded in any clinical research trial. Sometimes a trial had to be stopped if they were deemed serious enough to be putting lives at risk, but things weren't always as clear cut in the real world. The events were often coincidental and could be traced back to other factors. It cost billions of pounds to get a drug to market, with many of them failing in the early trial stages. Pharmaceutical companies accepted their losses based on the eventual breakthroughs that performed strongly.

"Earl likes her, though," Pearl continued. "She's stable, intelligent and ambitious, but she's unambiguous in the way she interprets things, which Dr Stone doesn't always agree with."

Darrell observed the interaction between Earl and Carol once more. Despite the good news that Carol North and Tia Stone had clashed, his guaranteed promotion appeared not to be the done deal he'd thought it was.

Chapter 2

The third cup of coffee Darrell gulped down his throat didn't help settle his anxiety. He was vacillating between fear and anger, and these were made much worse when the rest of the party joined him and Pearl. His heart was pounding in his chest, but not in a good way.

Carol North made a beeline and sat next to him.

"Hi. We didn't see you sitting over here."

Like hell you didn't, thought Darrell, but said, "Pearl and I have been soaking in the atmosphere since we got a message to meet up here. I'd hoped to see a bit more of the city before we gathered, but I guess it can't be helped." Darrell took another swig of coffee, trying to ease his dry throat, although the caffeine wasn't helping his heart rate. He couldn't get enough saliva into his mouth, which felt like sandpaper. He worried his lips might lock together.

"We'll all get a chance for some sightseeing before joining the coach, although we managed to see a bit of

Mumbai yesterday. We've been getting to know each other." Carol nodded towards the other scientists she and Earl had been talking to. She had a way of looking down her snub-nose when she spoke, an issue more apparent now they were face-to-face.

Carol wasn't bad looking, with sandy-brown hair and a beauty spot above the right upper lip. Her light blue eyes were flirting with his, but she was his chief competitor and not to be trusted. From what Darrell had witnessed, she and the other SRSs certainly appeared tight. The paranoid version of himself wondered if there had been a deliberate plot to push him to the fringes.

"So have we," he returned, smiling at Pearl who the other three were ignoring, sharing some joke between themselves. This meeting felt all wrong, but he was used to competition and would ride it out. Now he was alert to the threat, he wouldn't let them blindside him again. His ambition always won through in the end. He still had Tia Stone's confidence in him to rely on.

Close up, Carol was shorter than he'd imagined at about five-six, which should make it more difficult for her to appear so superior, although it didn't seem to stop her trying. Her shiny hair hung loosely on the shoulders. She wore a light cotton floral dress and a white jacket. By the way she and her group were all dressed in smart casual or business wear, he suspected they had known about this morning's meeting long before he and Pearl.

Carol ogled his hairy knees. "Where had you planned on going to then, the beach?"

There was the belittling tone again. Nevertheless, he could tell from the way she kept her eyes on his legs, she liked what she saw. He might be able to use it to his advantage.

He shrugged. "Can't say I'd made any grand plans," he replied. "I was just getting into the holiday spirit."

Carol's cheeks reddened when she realised he had noticed her looking at his legs. She tore her eyes away. Darrell grinned inwardly.

"Did you hear Tia's joining us?" Lizzie Meeton was by far the best looking of the group with long bleached-blonde hair and legs to die for. She was wearing a provocative yellow miniskirt. If he didn't know better, she could easily draw his eye away from the task at hand, but Darrell had observed her in meetings and was pretty certain she was ruthless underneath the dizzy blonde exterior. Seeing her in the flesh, though, he suspected she might be hard to resist.

"Really?" Pearl shot Darrell a 'told you so' look.

"Yes, Earl's just been telling us. He's coming along too."

Darrell groaned inwardly.

"I didn't realise you were on first-name terms with Dr Stone and Mr Spence." There was a sharp edge to Pearl's voice, something she had never revealed in meetings. She was as annoyed as Darrell at being left out, of that he was certain.

"I can't believe we're all here, and heading off on a luxury cruise. I say we party the time away." Matthew

Wright had sparkling brown eyes and brown shoulder-length hair, which he usually tied up. "We can continue where we left off last night." Darrell didn't miss the suggestive look Matthew sent in Carol's direction.

"You guys have already toured the city and met up last night?" Darrell had been outmanoeuvred, and he knew it.

"Yeah, didn't you two get the message?" Matthew asked.

"Soz, I forgot to add them to the group," said Lizzie, examining her painted gel nails.

Yeah, sure, thought Darrell.

Lizzie continued with the fingernail checking before asking nonchalantly, "Where's Sangita? I'm sure she said she'd be here early."

"Not after the amount she drank last night," said Gary Jacobs. Based in Dublin, Gary was the only one who wasn't among the competition for promotion. Relatively new, inexperienced and not yet a senior, he didn't present a threat as far as Darrell was concerned. It would be important to get him onside, though, and make use of his disarming popularity.

"Doesn't Sangita live in Mumbai?" Darrell checked.

"Yes, but we were all told about this meeting last night," said Lizzie. "She'll be here."

Told by whom? Darrell wanted to shout, but instead excused himself to go to the gents. While inside the shiny marble-floored restroom, he washed his face, swallowed a couple of painkillers, risking water from the tap, and chewed an antacid. Once he was done, he checked himself in the mirror, noticing how tense his jaw was. His mom had always known when he was annoyed; the jaw was a dead giveaway. She had taught him tension relieving facial exercises, which he performed while staring at his reflection.

"You've got this," he told himself. "The job is almost yours, just don't do anything stupid. Play the nice guy and don't get caught off guard." The pep talk bolstered his confidence and his jaw felt more relaxed.

He pulled the phone from his pocket and called the tuk-tuk driver to let him know the tour was off. Once that was done, he gave the peace stone nestling in his other pocket a few rubs before heading back to face the lions. He entered the lobby and saw the entire group was assembled, including Dr Stone, Earl Spence and Sangita Regum.

Darrell had a week to charm his boss, show her how capable he was and sweep aside his competitors. If it was a battle they wanted, then game on. Darrell was so focused on making the right approach, he didn't see the case before careering into it. Forcing himself not to curse about the pain in his shin, he glared up to berate the person who had left it there. The glare turned to a wide-eyed stare when he gazed into the most beautiful blue eyes he'd ever seen.

"I'm so sorry." The tall blonde woman's mouth was moving, but Darrell couldn't hear her words. He was besotted.

"Pardon?" He gathered himself together. Sangita was looking at him curiously, but he didn't care. "Oh... No problem. It's me who should apologise. I wasn't looking where I was going."

"As long as you're okay; your shin took quite a bashing."

"Hey, I'm fine." His heart leapt when he saw the luggage label on her suitcase. "Looks like we're gonna be on the same cruise."

"Are you joining the *Coral Queen*?" she asked.

"Yep. Perhaps you could repay me for my damaged shin by joining me for a drink once we're on board. I'm Darrell, Darrell Baker." He held out his hand.

Hesitation flickered in the deep blue eyes as she shook his hand. "I'm not sure I—"

"A friendly drink, I mean," he cut her off before she could refuse him. "I'm travelling with work colleagues. We're on a team-building exercise." Darrell hoped he wasn't sounding as keen as he felt. Women like her needed time, and he was prepared to give it to her.

"In that case, I'm sure we could have a drink." Her smile lit up the room.

Controlling an insane desire to pull her into his arms right now, he asked, "How will I find you?"

"Don't worry; I'll find you, Darrell Baker."

Even the way she said his name sent shivers down his spine. With the jaw exercises having come in handy, he grinned.

"I guess I'll have to take your word on that." He shot her his most innocent smile. "Do I get a name?"

"It's Rachel. I'm sorry, I really must go, I'm meeting a friend. See you on board."

You most certainly will, Rachel. Now he had two missions to accomplish in seven days. His priority was to convince Tia Stone he was the right man for the job. The second task was to spend as much of his downtime with the beautiful woman called Rachel as he could. He had every confidence she would succumb; women always fell for him. His mom said he had irresistible appeal, something he was determined to put to work the next time he met Rachel.

Sangita gave him a wary nod when he joined the group, but he was feeling confident and self-assured following his latest encounter. Sangita was the youngest and newest of the scientists, so he didn't think she would be too much trouble, but her father was wealthy and that could mean influential. He'd only discovered this by chance when reading an article about Muhmad Regum on the flight over. That type of wealth could buy a lot of favours, so Darrell would make sure he didn't underestimate her.

"Hi, good to see ya," he gave her a cheery greeting before taking the last seat. Earl Spence had taken Darrell's earlier one.

Tia Stone gave him a warm smile. "Now we're all here." Earl Spence was less friendly, but he would be like that with everyone except Carol North, from what Darrell had seen so far. For someone in PR, Earl could really do with brushing up on his people skills. Darrell suspected he was only in the job because of his relationship with Tia. Whatever that was.

No matter the reason, there was obviously work to be done with him.

Chapter 3

Rachel Jacobi-Prince threw her arms around her best friend, Sarah. The thrill of arriving in Mumbai the night before had shaken off some of the disappointment of Carlos not being able to join her on a trip they had both looked forward to.

"Rachel!" Sarah let go of her, stood a few steps back while doing a happy dance on the spot, which caused some heads to turn. The fact her friend was oblivious to the attention was one of the things Rachel loved about her.

"Sarah, it's so good to see you. I've missed you so much." The two women embraced again as only close friends could. Rachel blinked away a tear threatening to ruin the reunion.

Releasing her for the second time, Sarah said, "Come on, we're going on a sightseeing tour of Mumbai, and tonight Jason and I are treating you to an exotic dinner. Bernard's threatening to come along if he can persuade

Brigitte to cover for him. Put your suitcase over there with the others. The coach driver's loading them up. We don't have to be back until five o'clock. Then he'll take us to the ship, so we've got six hours to ourselves." Sarah was almost tripping over her words. Her brown eyes lit up when she was excited, giving them a shiny hue.

"You're the boss." Rachel followed her friend and happily left the large suitcase with the driver, who took it immediately and loaded it onto the waiting coach.

"Who was that good-looking guy I saw you talking to when I came in?" Sarah asked.

"Who do you mean? There are so many," Rachel teased.

"Ha-ha, seriously, who is he?"

"Just someone I bumped into – or rather, he bumped into my suitcase. He's one of your passengers. Darrell Baker, he said his name was. He's asked me to join him for a drink sometime."

"Of course he has," said Sarah, smirking. "You've still got it, Rachel Jacobi-Prince."

Rachel let out a heavy sigh. "Well, I wish it – whatever *it* is – would go somewhere else. Hopefully, he'll forget all about it. He told me he was with work colleagues on a team-building holiday." Rachel nodded discreetly towards the assembled group.

"Ah, I guess that must be the lot staying on the VIP floor. You know the one; it's where you and Marjorie went fishing for information after Lady Fanston died on your last cruise."

Sarah was referring to her last cruise when she had sailed with her octogenarian friend, Lady Marjorie Snellthorpe. "I wouldn't put it quite like that. And how do you know anyway? You were on your marriage furlough."

On the previous cruise, Rachel had discovered a part of the ship she'd never been to before: a VIP annexe with its own outside pool, a bar and a suite of rooms.

"You can't keep anything hidden on board the *Coral Queen*. You should know that by now. It was one of the first things Bernard told me when I got back. He just couldn't wait to tell me how, even when I'm not on board, you end up investigating murders. I was sorry to hear about Lady Fanston, though. I understand Marjorie knew her."

"Not well, but yes, it was all very sad. Anyway, tell me more about your VIP guests." Rachel turned to look once more at Darrell Baker and his friends. Sarah worked as a nurse on board the *Coral* and was privy to passenger details, although she didn't discuss anything confidential unless there was a murder to be solved.

"They work for a pharmaceutical company. I only heard about them because their CEO is meeting with Graham tomorrow."

"Trying to peddle their wares?"

"I guess so. The company is called Rejuvenescence Pharma. They specialise in age-defying pharmaceuticals or something of that ilk. It wouldn't be anything Graham is interested in stocking, but he likes to keep up to date with new initiatives, so he agreed to take the meeting."

Dr Graham Bentley was the chief medical officer on board the *Coral Queen*, and a man Rachel had grown fond of over the years.

"I have a feeling Marjorie wouldn't approve of trying to defy nature."

Sarah nodded. "If you go down that route, where would it end? Doesn't all medical treatment defy nature?"

"Good point," said Rachel. "Except in Marjorie's case; she believes you're better off staying as far away from doctors as possible, despite having her own private physician." They both chuckled at the enigma that was Marjorie Snellthorpe.

"Anyway, that's enough about your new friend and his gang, unless you've developed a wandering eye."

"Nope," said Rachel. "He seemed a nice chap, though. American, I think."

Sarah took Rachel's arm and led her outside into the busy metropolis. They almost crashed into a group of women and children circling them and holding out begging bowls. Sarah put a few coins into each bowl, and then marshalled Rachel towards a rickshaw.

The sights and sounds beyond the closed doors of the hotel assaulted all the senses. Noise from cars' honking horns and revving engines, along with crowds of people everywhere, was mesmerising. The heat and the smell of spices intermingling with rotting food took some getting used to, but then there was the taste of salt from the sea in the air, bringing welcome respite.

Sarah nudged her. "I told the rickshaw rider we are going to the Gateway of India, and then on to Elephanta Island. Is that all right with you?"

"Both sound great to me. How do you get used to this noise?"

"You don't. But I've learned from experience to enjoy it. Mumbai's a thriving city and home to Bollywood. This is the best mode of transport if you don't want to sit in traffic surrounded by angry drivers."

The rickshaw rider weaved niftily in and out of traffic – sometimes dangerously so – as they headed further away from the hotel.

"The car drivers spend a lot of time on their horns," Rachel shouted above the noise of yet another one blasting.

Sarah threw her head back, laughing happily. "I love India. It has some of the most amazing culture in the world, and yet it shocks every sense. I wish I could take you to a Bollywood movie while we're here, but I thought you'd prefer food over film."

"You thought right. I want to taste Indian food as we should taste it, rather than recipes that have been westernised to suit our palate."

"And so you shall, my friend. Look. We're almost there." Sarah pointed towards a grand structure with minarets on four corners of a central arch.

The rickshaw driver pulled in next to a large cobbled courtyard and Sarah paid him in rupees.

"How do you know how much to pay?" asked Rachel.

Sarah shot her a confused glance. "Didn't you hear me negotiating the price before we got in?"

"I couldn't hear anything for the noise." The truth was Rachel hadn't been paying much attention, yearning for holidays gone by when Carlos was by her side. She wanted them to share this experience. He would love it here.

Sarah didn't seem convinced but said nothing. "They call it the Gateway of India because it's the first thing you see when arriving by sea. It was like a welcome to Bombay, as it was called back then."

"Now it's a welcome to Mumbai."

"Exactly. Come on. Let's take a walk, then we'll get a boat over to the island."

They strolled across cobblestones towards the dominant feature. Rachel lost herself, soaking up the history of the grand arches towering over the large square. She read her guidebook and discovered the gateway had been built to commemorate King George V's earlier visit to Bombay in 1911. The monument wasn't actually built until thirteen years later, in 1924.

There were plenty of tourists around taking in the atmosphere, and multitudes of street traders trying to sell them their wares. Rachel bought a model rickshaw created out of bronzed wire. It was delicate, so she put it in her padded shoulder bag.

"Dad will love the workmanship of that. He's started a new hobby: making things out of castaways. His shed's now full of stuff that people in the village would normally toss out."

"I bet your mum loves that!"

"She calls it junk. He calls it upcycling. As long as it doesn't spill into the vicarage, she'll be fine with it. It might be a fad."

"Hasn't he got enough to do?" Sarah laughed before putting a hand to her mouth. "Did I ever thank him for officiating at our wedding?"

Rachel giggled. "Now who's not concentrating? Of course you did. He was glad to do it. I forgot to tell you, your mum sent a message via Dad to say you're to make sure Jason eats properly now you're married."

Sarah rolled her eyes. "Come on, there's the ferry. I prebooked our tickets."

Rachel noticed a few people from the hotel boarding the ferry when she took her seat. "I think we've got your pharmaceutical guests on board."

Sarah turned to look at them boarding. "I don't see your new admirer."

"Me neither. He might have already boarded."

Sarah nudged her. "You're not tempted, are you?"

"Not at all. They look interesting, that's all. I can already see they're a mismatched bunch, which could lead to a few sparks."

"We get enough argy-bargy on board, so I'll give them a miss if you don't mind." Sarah lost interest in the pharmaceutical group and they caught up on news about mutual friends. Rachel thought her friend appeared to have something on her mind, and Rachel certainly had a lot on her own, but this wasn't the place to discuss either concern.

Once they arrived at the pier, Sarah led the way to a set of stone steps. Rachel noticed the pharma group boarding a miniature train to take them up the steep incline. Darrell was with them, talking to a woman with long, wavy black hair. She looked around forty and wore designer clothes. The woman carried what looked like a Gucci handbag.

Either they earn a lot of money, or she's the boss, thought Rachel.

"Are you ready?" Sarah asked. "There's a hundred and twenty-five steps to climb. At the top, we get to the cave temples."

"I'll race you."

Sarah frowned. "No way. You jog up if you want to; I'm walking."

Rachel conceded and walked with her friend, who was breathless by the time they reached the caves. "You're out of condition," she teased.

"I'm not an adrenaline junkie like you."

After examining an enormous statue of Shiva with three faces, they entered through an arch into one of the caves. Inside, noises echoed back and forth, making it difficult to know where the sounds originated. They ambled through the caves for a short time. The deeper they got, the quieter it became.

Until they heard a shrill scream.

Chapter 4

"Are you all right?"

Sarah got to the sandy-haired woman ahead of Rachel. Steps leading to more caves on a higher level rose from where the woman was seated on the bottom step, examining her tanned knees for damage.

"I'm fine." The woman had an upturned nose that made her appear to be looking down on them, even though her head was lower than both theirs. Her accent was Northern Irish. "No harm done."

Rachel imagined the fall bruised her ego more than her knees, and her white cotton jacket would probably need specialist cleaning.

"Here. Let me help you." Sarah offered the woman an arm. "I'm Sarah, this is Rachel."

"Carol, Carol North," she said, taking Sarah's arm. She examined the sleeve of her jacket and sniffed before looking at them. "Thanks for helping me out."

"The steps are uneven. It's easily done," said Sarah.

"What? Oh yes, they are." Carol looked back up the steps. "I could have sworn I felt someone push me." She shivered before giving a nervous laugh. "Caves freak me out at the best of times. Do you know where the entrance is?"

"That way." Rachel pointed towards people milling around further back. "Are you on holiday?"

"Yeah, I'm going on a cruise."

"Small world. So are we."

"Are you on the *Coral Queen*?" Carol asked.

Rachel nodded. "We might see you again, then."

"You never know. We're sort of working, but I might see you around. Thanks again."

They watched her until she disappeared from view. "She must be one of the Rejuvenescence group," said Sarah. "Did you recognise her?"

"No. I only noticed a few of them, but you're right. It can't be coincidence that another youngish businessperson is taking a cruise for work."

"You'd be surprised. Although few companies would fly their employees out to India."

Rachel ran up the steps Carol had stumbled down and took a quick look around. There were people in the distance but no-one nearby. With a maze of passages, it was impossible to guess from which way Carol North had approached the steps.

Rachel spotted a shadow along the passage to the right.

"Surely you don't think someone really pushed her?" Sarah arrived at her side. By the time Rachel looked back towards the place where she had seen the shadow, it had gone. She, like Carol had, shivered.

"I doubt it. Perhaps she's got an overactive imagination. It's easy to dream up things with all this spirituality around."

"She's silly, straying away from her group. There's always safety in numbers," said Sarah. Rachel had the feeling that it might be someone in the group Carol had to fear, rather than mysterious ogres in the dark.

"Shall we get back? I'd like to see a bit more of the promenade around the Gateway before we head to the ship."

"Okay. The ferries run every half hour, so we should be able to get one. I tell you what, I'll treat you to a coffee at the Taj Mahal Restaurant."

"We're a bit far away from the Taj Mahal, aren't we?" Rachel teased.

"You're really not your usual observant self, Rachel. It's the ginormous hotel across the road from the Gateway. You can't miss it."

Rachel took her friend's arm. "Evidently I did. Lead on, Stanley."

"Oh, we're Livingstone and Stanley rather than Holmes and Watson today, are we?" Sarah replied, tittering.

"As we're exploring another continent, I felt it apt," Rachel replied.

They just made it onto a ferry ready to depart. Once back in the square in Mumbai, Rachel could see why Sarah had been so surprised she hadn't noticed the imposing Taj Mahal Hotel. Totally engrossed in admiring the architecture while navigating the cobblestones, she almost missed hearing a car speeding up towards her.

Rachel's reactions were lightning quick as she leapt into action, pushing a man out of the car's path and landing on top of him. The car sped away as fast as it had arrived.

"What just happened?" A pale Darrell Baker lay on the ground with Rachel still on top of him, but she wasn't looking in his direction.

"Rachel!" Sarah helped her up while Darrell's party gathered around him.

"That guy mounted the pavement," said Rachel, shocked. "The car was heading straight for you," she explained as Darrell stood up, wiping down his shorts.

"You must have really cheesed someone off, mate," said a younger man with curly fair hair and a goatee beard.

Darrell wasn't smiling. He was trembling but doing his best to hide it from his colleagues.

"It seems I'm indebted to you," he said to Rachel.

"It was nothing."

"Quick reflexes you've got," said a leggy blonde woman.

"Be careful in India. Drivers will do anything to dodge the traffic." Rachel examined the latest speaker, a young Asian woman wearing a turquoise silk blouse and matching skirt. She had noticed her in the hotel earlier.

"And do they make a habit of mounting pavements and accelerating into pedestrians?" Rachel stared into the woman's deep brown eyes.

"I'm just saying. You should be careful before jumping into traffic. Next time you might not be so lucky."

Rachel didn't like the woman's attitude but let it go.

Sarah took her arm. "I think it's time for that coffee." She steered Rachel away from the pharma group. As soon as they were out of earshot, she stammered, "W-what were you thinking, Rachel? That woman's right: that car could have killed you."

Now the adrenaline burst was waning, Rachel felt exhausted. "It all happened so quickly. I reacted instinctively. You'd have done the same thing."

Sarah must have recognised the aftershock setting in because she didn't give Rachel any more reprimands. "That driver's a maniac. I should have got his plates."

Rachel had been thinking the same thing, although something told her it would have been pointless. "Now we know Darrell and Carol are in the same group. They're either cursed or someone dangerous is out to get them. One accident I can accept but two near-misses in one day? I hope they've got good insurance cover. Carol North could have imagined being pushed, but that car swerved off the road towards Darrell."

"Why would anyone in India want to run over a tourist or push someone down the steps?"

Sarah has a point, Rachel thought while forcing her legs one in front of the other to move towards the hotel.

"I suppose it could have been a random accident; a drug or drunk driver. It would explain why they didn't stop. Plus, it's not unheard of for a person to press on the accelerator instead of the brake. Did you see the driver?"

"No. It could have been a woman. My guess is it was random."

"You're right, Sarah. When I worked in traffic, I came across plenty of incidents, usually when someone was using a mobile phone while driving. And maybe that woman's right, too. The driving in Mumbai leaves a lot to be desired."

***

After a calming hour in the grandest hotel she had ever been inside, Rachel was almost convinced the Darrell incident was nothing more than the result of someone pressing hard on the wrong pedal because they were either on the phone or drunk. She and Sarah returned to the original hotel just in time to board the coach still parked outside.

"I've got to say, I'm pleased the ship is staying in Mumbai overnight. I'm looking forward to seeing this city lit up," said Rachel when they arrived at the port.

"Me too. I'll meet you at eight. I have to board via the servants' entrance." Sarah laughed and Rachel groaned, seeing lines of people waiting to check in and board.

"At least you won't be in that queue."

"No doubt you'll meet another admirer," Sarah yelled over her shoulder as she left Rachel and headed for the crew's gangway.

"Not funny, Nurse Bradshaw. Not funny at all." Sarah, like Rachel, had kept her maiden name for work purposes. They had both chosen to go double-barrelled for married life, Rachel because she loved the name Prince and Sarah because she was an only child and wanted to continue the family surname.

Rachel was still smiling at Sarah's comment when she joined the back of a queue of passengers. She noticed the pharma group passing through the VIP entrance, none of them looking happy, but judging by the near-miss they had witnessed, she wasn't surprised. Rachel saw Carol nearest the front, chatting to an older man with silver hair and a moustache. The long-legged blonde woman was engrossed in conversation with a woman in her forties, who had dark brown hair cut in a bob. The slim, fair-haired man who had tried to make a joke about the accident earlier appeared to be teasing Darrell, who was glaring at the leggy blonde.

Rachel shrugged, resigned to the wait while watching the pharma group hurry through security and onto the ship. She grinned from ear to ear when she caught sight of Bernard, one of Sarah's nursing colleagues, in the passenger lounge next door to the check-in lounge, and hoped he would join them for dinner. He was a lot of fun.

She compared the nursing team with the pharma team. One happy and functional, the other miserable and most likely dysfunctional.

Chapter 5

Still reeling from the morning's meeting and his lucky escape from being mowed down, Darrell waited on the dockside for the others to meet him. He had arrived early, determined to give a good account of himself this evening.

Gary, or Gaz as he had insisted on being called, arrived first with a wide grin on his face. His greeting was genuine.

"Hiya, have you settled in okay after all the excitement?"

"Excitement isn't what I would have called it, but yep, I've unpacked." Darrell grimaced, still sore from being sent flying to the ground by Rachel. Not quite what he'd had in mind for their next meeting, but the thought of it brought a smile to his face. "Any idea where we're going tonight?"

"Sangita's booked us a table at a restaurant where she says we can taste proper Indian food. It's in the city and I suppose, as she lives here, we have to take her word for it when she promises it will be a culinary treat. I'm a big fan of Indian food. We've got some excellent restaurants in Dublin sure enough, but I bet they're nothing like the real thing. Dabbled at cooking it meself; I fancy meself as a bit of a chef in me spare time. My girlfriend says I'm wasted in pharmaceuticals. Do yer like cooking yerself?"

"I can't say it's something I'm into. I've been too long in New York, and we Americans eat out more than we eat in. At least, this Americanised Englishman does."

"I couldn't quite tell from the accent."

"I'm lucky enough to have dual nationality. My mom's English, but my dad's American. I was born in London and lived there until I finished primary school, then we moved to New York with my dad's work."

"So, when you're not being run over, what are you into?"

Darrell winced at the second reminder of his near-miss. The question was simple enough, but he found he couldn't answer it. Apart from the odd bit of socialising, all he ever did was work. That's why he'd hoped to explore Mumbai on his own today. He needed a break, otherwise ambition would consume his every waking hour. Now his dreams were being threatened by a bunch of people he hadn't expected would impede his route to the top. He felt like a steam train that's found itself at the station without coal to continue its journey.

Gaz was still waiting for an answer, so he shrugged. "I play the odd video game."

"Really? I can't say I've ever taken to that sort of stuff. It's not my thing. The only reason I took this job is 'cos it pays well and me mam and dad want me to get me own place. After all that malarky this morning, I'll be happy to let my hair down. What did you make of the lecture?"

Darrell was cautious. "I guess we're gonna have to prove ourselves worthy of the boss's request."

"It all seems barmy to me. It's not as if we work together… not really. I'm in Dublin, you're in New York. The others are all over the shop as well. If you ask me, it's overkill, but I'll not be complaining about the location – I'll take a team-building holiday on a luxury cruise liner, all expenses paid, any day."

The man with the goatee beard was growing on Darrell. Gaz didn't appear to be as snarky as the rest of the group, and was nearer Darrell's own age. Perhaps he would indeed turn out to be an ally.

"You've got a point there. What do you think of Mumbai so far?"

"I enjoyed the caves. There was something about them, otherworldly like. I'm a Catholic meself – lapsed, mind – but once a Catholic, always a Catholic, that's what me mam says. What about you?"

"I'm not religious."

"No. I meant, what do you make of the city?"

"I like it. Apart from the drivers, and the smell."

"I can't say I'm a fan of the crowds," said Gaz.

"You'd hate New York then. Here are the others now." Darrell felt like someone had thumped him in the stomach when he saw Earl Spence among the company. *Is that man not going to leave us alone for one minute?*

Gaz lowered his voice. "I hope he's not coming. I was looking forward to downing the local booze with no-one breathing down me neck."

"Good evening, boys," Earl sounded more cheerful than he had been when he and Tia Stone had delivered the bombshell this morning before sending them off to explore the city. Perhaps he'd been sampling the ship's cocktails.

"Hi," Darrell offered his widest smile.

Sangita sprinted in front of the others. "I suggest we take two taxis. You're in for a tantalising feast tonight."

"So I hear," said Darrell.

"Come on then, I'm starved." Gaz laughed merrily.

They headed through port security where a clamour of taxis, rickshaws and tuk-tuks hustled. The noise made it difficult to hear himself think, but Darrell was hot on the trail of Sangita, determined to get into the same taxi with her and Earl, who appeared to have abandoned Carol and was now glued to the younger woman's side. He needed the opportunity to prove himself, and Sangita was turning into a bigger threat than he'd first thought.

Gaz also made it into the lead taxi.

"Just tell your driver to follow us," Sangita told the frowning Lizzie.

Lizzie Longlegs. Darrell grinned to himself. That would be her nickname from now on.

"Will Dr Stone be joining us?" Gaz asked Earl the question Darrell had wanted answering.

"She might come along later after making some business calls if she has time. I'm sure she'll call me if she can make it."

Sangita sat in the front and spoke to the driver in Hindi, so none of the others had a clue where they were heading. As soon as they got into the busier part of the city, the sound of car horns honking loudly and incessantly made it impossible to speak, as well as making Darrell nervous. The driver had his window wound down, so it was noisier than ever. Darrell tried not to show how disgusted he was by the stench of rotting food, cow dung and sewerage.

"Is it always like this?" Gaz asked.

"Noisy, you mean?" Sangita checked.

"Yeah, and smelly."

Darrell noticed a half-smile cross Earl's face.

"It's always bad at this time of year because of the heat, but it's worse in the full summer. We have problems with pollution."

Understatement of the year, thought Darrell, trying to breathe through his mouth rather than his nose. The thick yellow smog was irritating his lungs.

Sangita noticed him struggling and said something to the driver, who wound his window up.

"So where exactly are we? Crikey!" Darrell yelled as the taxi driver slammed on the brakes. His head rushed towards the passenger seat, but he just managed to stop himself from headbutting the back rest by throwing his hands forward. "What the…"

"Cows are sacred in India," explained Sangita, looking back over her shoulder. "They have the right of way, although they rarely roam in this part of the city." She turned to the taxi driver again and said something in Hindi. The taxi driver laughed a deep belly laugh. Somehow, Darrell suspected he was the butt of the joke.

"Had you done your research, you would know to fasten your seatbelt," Earl's condescending tone had returned.

Darrell didn't reply. He was trying to block flashbacks from this afternoon overwhelming his mind. His attempt at being friendly wasn't going to plan.

"He couldn't do it up. It's broke," said Gaz, coming to his rescue. When he got the promotion, Darrell would see that Gaz was one of his trusty sidekicks.

Once the cows blocking the route shifted enough for the driver to manoeuvre around them, Gaz distracted Earl by pointing at a group of Buddhist monks.

"I've gotta get me one of those orange outfits."

Earl smirked. "We'll see what we can do."

"We're almost there," Sangita again looked over her shoulder at them squashed up in the back seat. "Comfortable, boys?" She winked audaciously at Earl, whose eyes popped.

So that's how it is. What would Sangita do to get a chance at his promotion? Darrell felt a nudge in his ribs from Gaz, who was sitting in the centre. As soon as the car stopped and they were outside, Gaz motioned sticking a finger down his throat.

"She wouldn't sleep with the old guy, surely?"

Darrell put his finger to his lips as the other two approached after Earl had paid the driver. The second taxi pulled up right behind them and the other four got out. Lizzie was tight-lipped, glaring at Sangita who was still flirting with Earl. Pearl raised her eyebrows, while Carol and Matthew didn't seem to notice.

The second taxi driver yelled something.

"He wants to be paid," said Sangita.

"How much?" Matthew Wright's hand dug into his pocket, pulling out a bundle of notes.

"Put that away, idiot!" said Lizzie. "Do you want us all to be robbed?"

"Allow me," said Earl.

"Although not all Indians are thieves." Sangita shot Lizzie a glare. "You have to be careful as some criminals watch out for drunken tourists. Anyway, I think you'll like it here. It's a well-established and popular Goan restaurant."

They stood in the street for a few minutes, taking in their surroundings and looking at the sign: O Pedro. Darrell stood back and whistled.

"Sounds Spanish to me. Was Goa a Spanish colony? Mumbai reminds me a bit of New York."

"Many people say that," said Sangita, ignoring his question. As she led the way across the road, Lizzie Meeton and Carol North accosted Earl.

Matt joined the other two men. "Sangita told us earlier it's the go-to place for Goan cuisine."

"We should *Go An* eat then," said Darrell, still watching Earl.

Sangita turned and laughed at his joke. "Yes, let's do that." She took a few strides towards the door. The waiter welcomed her.

"Something tells me she's no stranger here," said Darrell.

Gaz gave a nod. "That explains why we're at a Goan restaurant in Mumbai when we'll be in Goa the day after tomorrow. Boy, would you look at that geezer?" He pointed to Earl. "He's lapping up the attention. The guy's far too old for any of the gals here, even Pantoni."

Darrell concurred. Earl Spence had to be sixty if he was a day. Supposedly happily married with grownup kids, he was behaving like a grandad at a stag do.

"Well, won't you look at that?" Gaz's attention was suddenly turned elsewhere as he let out a low whistle. "I suggest we get away as soon as we can from this dreary lot."

Darrell followed his gaze and couldn't agree more. His heart skipped a beat when he saw the woman who had most likely saved his life throwing her head back, laughing at something the friend she'd been with this afternoon was saying.

"The blonde's mine," he said.

"Fine. They're both gorgeous," said Gaz. "Ain't she the woman who bowled you over earlier?"

"In more ways than one." Darrell felt himself relax.

"I say we let her choose."

"You forget I have the upper hand."

"Which is?"

"She's already agreed to have a drink with me."

"Fast mover," said Gaz.

The night had just got a whole lot better. But first, Darrell realised, there was work to be done.

Chapter 6

The restaurant Sarah and Jason had chosen was bustling with life. They had eaten three delicious courses of speciality food and Rachel felt full to bursting. Bernard and Jason were at the bar getting drinks, leaving Rachel and Sarah to enjoy watching the vibrant night world of India through the windows. Each time someone opened the door, they were treated to a cacophony that arrived or left with them. The aromas of delicious food perfusing the restaurant mostly disguised street smells, and burning incense sticks dealt with any attempting to intrude.

"My travel book says that Mumbai is often compared to New York; I can see why," remarked Rachel.

"They do have similarities," said Sarah, "although the pollution is much worse here. I think you'll agree, after that meal, the food is infinitely better in Mumbai."

Rachel patted her stomach. "I'll let the paunch speak for itself. That Prawn Who-Maan was delicious. I don't remember ever tasting anything so good."

Sarah grinned. "Bernard's love is the fish curry. He says it reminds him of the Pinoy fish curry his wife cooks when he's home in Manila."

"Bernard must miss his family." Rachel sighed.

"Look, Rachel. I haven't asked before because I wanted to give you time, but is something wrong? You're not quite yourself."

Rachel had thought she was doing a great job of hiding her worries. Her act would have been good enough for most people, but she and Sarah had known each other since they were children and Sarah could read her. She gazed at her wedding band, twirling it round and round.

Sarah's hand flew to her face as her jaw dropped. "Oh no, Rachel. Is that why you were flirting back at the hotel with that guy you nearly got killed for? Please don't tell me you and Carlos are splitting up."

"I was not flirting with any guy, and no, of course we're not. We're fine," Rachel snapped before admitting, "Actually, it's worse than that."

"Now I'm seriously worried. What could be worse than splitting up with your husband?"

"Your husband being on a secret mission in China…" Rachel lowered her voice to a whisper. "Shush, the guys are on their way back. No-one must know, Sarah."

Rachel hoped it hadn't been a mistake mentioning where Carlos was. Top secrecy around his mission to

China was everything, but he would understand she had to speak to someone she could trust, otherwise anxiety would ruin her trip. Either way, it was too late now. Sarah would not let it go, and Rachel's annoyance with Carlos taking the mission was nothing compared to her worry about his safety.

Rachel had thought the cruise might help relieve her tension. There was still time; it was only the first day. At least now she would have someone to talk to.

Sarah had little time to hide her shocked expression, but as it turned out, she didn't need to. At the same time Jason and Bernard approached from one side, Darrell Baker and his blond friend appeared on the other.

Darrell helped himself to the chair next to Rachel.

"We've gotta stop meeting like this." Darrell's eyes were bloodshot, his speech slurred and his voice loud. "Would tonight be a good time to have that drink? This is my buddy, Gaz. I don't think you met properly when you were my guardian angel. He'd be thrilled to make it a foursome."

"NOW would not be a good time for a drink, and we're *already* a foursome." Jason placed drinks on the table, glaring down at Darrell's smiley companion who had just opened his mouth to speak to Sarah. It snapped shut again.

Darrell leapt up, stepping back from the table. "Sorry, dude. My mistake. Some other time, Rachel."

Rachel giggled at hearing the man with Darrell moaning, "I didn't realise they were married."

"I didn't know either," Darrell slurred in reply. "I bet you weren't going to mention your girlfriend, though, eh?" He poked his friend Gaz in the chest.

"Did you see the muscles of that guy?"

"Never mind, we'll just have to rejoin the others." Darrell bumped into a large man wearing a traditional long-sleeved brown sherwani with ornate gold buttons running down the front. The man looked none too pleased, afterwards brushing his shoulder with his hand as if it was contaminated.

"Who are those guys?" Jason took his seat, still scowling.

"*They* are passengers from our cruise ship, so no fisticuffs, Mr Security Officer." Sarah stroked Jason's arm. "Chill, Jason; they've had too much to drink, that's all. Besides, I think it's Rachel they're interested in, not me."

Jason was still glowering, eyes firmly fixed on the table where Darrell and Gaz had sat down with the rest of their party.

"I met the *very* drunk one at the hotel this morning. He was pleasant enough then, but he's obviously had way too much of the local liquor. He was just being overfriendly. Poor guy almost got run over this afternoon when Sarah took me to the Gateway of India." Rachel frowned at the memory.

"You were out with them?" Jason's eyes were now on Sarah.

"Of course not. They happened to be there, and he almost got in the way of an angry driver."

Rachel intervened, shooting Sarah a worried look about Jason's reaction. "Let's forget about it. They're just a pair of holidaymakers out for a good time."

Sarah shook her head, saying nothing more about either incident.

"Okay, I'll apologise to the guy if I see him again," said Jason, leaning over to kiss Sarah on the cheek.

"Nah, don't do that. He won't remember a thing come the morning," said Bernard. "And if he does, I'll give him one of my Stingers so he won't complain about our security staff." The jovial Filipino man laughed.

Sarah scrunched up her nose. "You might as well give him battery acid."

Bernard put a hand to his chest, smirking at the same time. "That hurts. It took me years to develop my secret recipe."

"And it's taken me years to recover from just one sip," mocked Sarah.

Bernard's Stinger cocktail was a love-hate thing. Some of the crew couldn't get enough of the blue drink and others, like Sarah, would never touch one again.

A noise in the corner distracted them as chairs scraped across the wooden floor. As one, the pharmaceutical group had all stood up. Some were less steady than others, namely Darrell. The woman with wavy black hair, whom Rachel had noticed on Elephanta Island, had entered. Around Rachel's height, she wore a close-fitting above-the-knee white dress.

"She must be the boss, Dr Tia Stone," said Bernard. "If she's the one meeting with Graham tomorrow, Gwen might have competition."

Sarah punched Bernard's arm. "Stop it."

Pretend-rubbing his arm, Bernard replied, "What? I didn't say anything. You should tell your wife not to be such a bully, Jason."

Jason held his palms up, forcing a smile. "You deserve everything you get, mate. I'm not getting involved."

"So Gwen and Graham are an item?" Rachel quizzed.

"We think so, but it's not official," said Sarah. "And it's none of our business." She gave Bernard a warning look and the smaller man shrugged. "You're right, though. That's Dr Tia Stone. I looked her up. She's fifty, according to Wiki—"

"Never!" said Bernard. "She only looks around forty."

Rachel, too, was surprised at the revelation. Tia Stone looked much younger than fifty.

"Then she must take her own medicine because she's definitely fifty. She's CEO of Rejuvenescence Pharma, a growing company that's recently floated on the stock exchange. She holds a doctorate in pharmacology from Cambridge and started the company from scratch. It launched on a value of around \$150m and went straight into the S&P 500."

"Get you," Bernard teased. "Since when did you take an interest in pharmaceutical companies?"

"Since Graham told me and Gwen about tomorrow's meeting first thing this morning – while you were still in bed, I might add. I looked her up. Graham thinks one of the bigger players will snap the company up because they've got a revolutionary new drug doing exceptionally well in clinical trials."

Rachel had been listening to the conversation while keeping one eye on Darrell and his colleagues. She hoped he wouldn't embarrass himself too much in front of his boss. The friction she had detected among his group would become worse when fuelled by alcohol. They were laughing and smiling, but it was tarnished by the occasional tight-lipped glare, particularly aimed at Darrell.

"They don't get on." Rachel spoke her thoughts out loud.

"I can explain why." Bernard chuckled. "Don't look at me like that, Sarah. I too have my spies."

Sarah gave an eye roll. "Don't we know it?" she said, grinning.

"I don't really have snoops, but I have a mole. One of them…" he lowered his voice "…Matthew Wright – the guy with the long brown hair – he's asthmatic; the pollution was getting to him, so he came to surgery before I got off duty. He's quite a chatterbox."

Jason nudged him. "You're itching to tell us, mate, so get it off your chest."

"Matthew's based in Cardiff. They're all based in different parts of the world, heading up research teams while the company expands. I think Dr Stone is based in Dublin."

"Yes, that's where the head office is," Sarah confirmed.

Rachel watched as the group left the restaurant before returning her attention to Bernard once more.

"And?"

"Oh yeah. Well, there's a promotion up for grabs. Your drunken admirer is favourite for it – the boss likes him, apparently – but the others are determined to put up a fight. The older guy has the boss's ear, and he prefers the women."

"I wonder why," Sarah's voice dripped sarcasm.

"Anything else?" asked Rachel.

"That's all I know. There's only so much a guy can ask while dishing out an inhaler. To be honest, I wouldn't have been interested at all if I hadn't heard his boss was coming to see Graham."

"Plus, you do like a bit of gossip," teased Jason.

"There is that," said Bernard. "On a more serious note, the guy Matthew... or was it Matt he said to call him? He said the promotion was a big deal and the virtual daggers were drawn. Let's hope they don't become real, or Rachel could have another murder on her hands."

Rachel thought again about the car mounting the pavement and felt a sense of foreboding settle like a lump in her stomach.

Surely not again?

Chapter 7

They had arrived back at the ship late the previous night and Rachel had headed straight to bed to escape the sultry air – grateful for the air-conditioning in every room – and give her body a chance to get over the jet lag. Some hope; she had been up half the night and woke early.

They would sail at 8am. Rachel pulled on a pair of shorts and a vest before heading up to deck sixteen for her morning jog. Sarah hadn't had any opportunity to quiz her further on the Carlos situation the night before and was working today, so she'd have to catch her later.

The air was already humid but not too hot; probably the best time to go for a run. Other early-bird passengers were out strolling, power-walking or running. Rachel noticed the older man from Darrell's group heading towards her. He stopped abruptly, blocking her path, huffing to catch his breath.

"Good morning," he offered. Huge dark lines beneath his eyes were a giveaway that he was suffering from the aftereffects of the night before. Rachel didn't want to stop running, but having stopped, she was too polite to start again, especially as it looked like he might keel over any minute.

"Are you all right?"

"Yeah fine; just wishing I'd got more sleep, that's all."

"I know what you mean. It's going to be another beautiful day, I think."

"India's too hot, even for a Texan." He wiped the sweat from his face. "I guess most people are sensible enough to be tucked up in bed."

"Apart from the crew." Rachel inclined her head towards the dockside, where members of the crew were getting things ready for departure. She laughed as a few stragglers rushed to get back aboard before it was too late. "And others might not have been to bed at all."

The man with silver hair and neatly trimmed moustache smiled for the first time, offering her his hand.

"Where are my manners? Earl Spence at your service, ma'am."

Rachel took the clammy hand as Earl Spence's dark green eyes stared at her over a pair of half-moon glasses. Despite the sweat, his grey t-shirt appeared to have just come out of the wrapping, creases and all. She guessed he was around sixty.

"Pleased to meet you, Earl. I'm Rachel."

A slight awkwardness followed while Earl cleared his throat.

"Is this your first cruise, sweetheart?"

Rachel cringed. "No. I've been on quite a few now. What about you?"

"I'm a cruise virgin. It's no vacation for me, though. I've gotta work."

"Oh? Poor you. I hope you get a little time to relax. India – I'm assured – is a beautiful country."

"That might be difficult. It's hard to wind down when I've got a bunch of ambitious guys and gals, most of 'em half my age, after the same job. My, er... boss is looking for a new right-hand man – or woman."

Not missing the reluctant use of the word boss, Rachel wondered if Earl himself would rather be in charge.

"I take it from what you said you're helping your boss decide."

"Sure am," he said, standing straight and puffing out his chest. "Without direction, she tends to go for the wrong type, and it's my job to make sure that doesn't happen. Whoever we choose has to be the right person; someone who won't damage the company's reputation. We're in pharmaceuticals, you see. Sometimes pharma companies get a bad press. Which makes it vital to get the right people at the top."

Rachel suspected Earl would be more interested in choosing someone who would march to his tune.

"I know little about pharmaceuticals. I've heard of a few companies, of course. Is yours a big company?"

"It's not as big as some, but it's fast-growing. We've got a major new drug in the pipeline." Earl's eyes sparkled for the first time. Unable to stop himself from rubbing his hands together, he looked almost childlike.

"How exciting," she said, torn between wanting to know more than Sarah had already told her and the need to finish her run before it got any hotter. "I hope it's a new cancer cure."

"Even better than that, Rachel..." Rachel thanked her stars he didn't use the term 'sweetheart' again. "It's a cure for ageing. I can't say too much, but that much has already been hinted at in the press. We are about to turn the idea of ageing on its head."

"I see," said Rachel, thinking once again that her dear octogenarian friend, Marjorie, might not approve of trying to interfere with nature. Personally, she couldn't help believing that anything that would help people like Marjorie – and Rachel's parents, for that matter – live longer would be a good thing. "I take it you mean people living healthily for longer?"

Earl tapped his nose. "You'll have to wait and see, sweetheart..." Rachel's heart sank, "... and keep an eye on the news for Rejuvenescence Pharma. We're going to change the way the world thinks about ageing. You can count on it."

An announcement over the ship's Tannoy interrupted their conversation. "This is a passenger announcement. Would Mr Darrell Baker report to reception. Mr Darrell Baker, please report to reception."

"What's that boy gone and done now?" Earl snapped. "He's one of ours. I'd better check on what's happening." Earl spun on his heels and headed for the nearest entrance to the ship's interior.

Rachel wondered why Darrell was being summoned to reception so early in the morning and hoped, for his sake, it wasn't bad news. With the patronising Earl Spence gone, she resumed her run.

Numerous other calls for Mr Darrell Baker during the thirty minutes prior to her returning to her room and the ship leaving got Rachel wondering even more. Once showered and changed, she watched the heavy ropes being released from their moorings. A captain's announcement letting them know they were about to sail, along with the weather forecast for the day, followed.

Rachel sat on her balcony, scanning her eyes along the gradually disappearing dock as the enormous ship eased away from the side. Leaving one destination and heading on to the next was one of the most exciting parts of cruising.

Rachel sat mesmerised for half an hour, watching people waving from the dock and returning the waves of children and adults on pleasure boats. It would have been nice to stay longer in Mumbai, although Rachel had found the dense population a little too much in her anxious state. A sudden rush of panic threatened to settle on her stomach, taking her by surprise.

"Stop this," she chastised herself. It was time to get some breakfast.

As she entered the buffet, Rachel smiled at a few of the staff she recognised while helping herself to cereal, toast and a pastry. She took her food to a table outside where her favourite Jamaican waiter, Joshua, was pushing his trolley, singing and serving hot drinks. He stopped at her table.

"Good to see you again, ma'am. How come you gets more beautiful as time passes?" His deep brown eyes twinkled in the sunlight.

"And how come you get more charming every time we meet?" she replied, laughing. "I see you haven't lost the gift of the gab." Joshua's singing and sunny disposition were always popular with passengers. He flirted with the women and bantered with the men as he did his morning drinks round.

He gave her a huge grin. "I didn't see you upstairs this fine morning."

"I was there, maybe a bit earlier than usual." Rachel had got to know Joshua on her first or second cruise because they both jogged. "How are the knees?"

"Holding up, ma'am. They're holding up. Now, what can I get ya this beautiful morning?"

"I'd love a strong coffee, please."

Joshua poured her drink. "There you go. How did you like Mumbai?"

"Beautiful. I might have to return for a longer stay with my husband. There's a lot to see."

"Indeed, there is always something going on back there. I take it you saw the Gateway? Hard to miss anyway."

"I did. It was beautiful. We also went to Elephanta Island, to the caves."

"Now that's an interesting place. Mumbai's a bit too busy for me, mind. I prefer the laid-back style of place, ya know? I miss me home sometimes. These big metropolises – they're too loud for my liking. Some as don't find their way back, ya know?"

Rachel's ears pricked up. "Don't tell me you've had crew disappear again?" It wasn't unheard of for crew on shore leave to drink too much, get carried away and miss a sailing. Cruise ships waited for no-one, unless passengers were on an organised bus tour.

"No, this time it's passengers that's gone walkabout."

Rachel felt a sense of foreboding, recalling all the announcements for Darrell earlier.

"Passengers, you say?"

Joshua shrugged. "I'm not so sure how many, but me heard rumours that at least one didn't show up this morning. Now, don't you get lost."

Joshua was singing again as he moved on to the next table. Rachel felt as though a tonne weight had been dropped on her stomach.

Chapter 8

Twenty minutes after finishing breakfast, Rachel was pacing outside the chief of security Jack Waverley's office, debating whether she should knock on the door or go away again. Just as she'd opted for the latter, the door opened and Jason's beaming smile greeted her, his expression changing to a confused frown within seconds.

"Hi, Rachel. Have you come to say hello to the chief?"

Rachel's throat tightened as Waverley appeared behind him.

"It's good to see you, Rachel. How are you?" The chief seemed genuinely happy to see her until she hesitated. "Please tell me this is a social call."

"Of course. What else would it be?"

"Something in your eye. I'm too long in the tooth to dance around while you get to the real reason you're here. You can't possibly have come across a crime already," Waverley forced a laugh mixed with a nervous cough.

"I'm not sure."

"What's on your mind?" he sighed.

The chief and Rachel had an unstable relationship. It could sometimes be described as a friendship, except it depended on whether she was helping or, in his opinion, hindering his investigations.

"Probably nothing," she said.

Waverley's right hand immediately stroked back the sparse hair on his forehead. "Which means it's probably something. I think you'd better come inside. You too, Goodridge."

"Yes, sir," said Jason.

Moments later, they were sitting around the coffee table in the security chief's office.

"Coffee?" Waverley asked.

Rachel smiled. "Yes please. I see you've had your office redecorated."

"Good of you to notice. It was Brenda's doing. She thought it was too drab and that it might be affecting my, erm…" the chief cleared his throat, "… mood."

Rachel thought it unlikely the new decor would help Waverley cope with the stress of his job, but it couldn't hurt. Brenda had chosen a modern pastel grey for the walls and a warmer green-speckled grey for the carpet. A canvas picture of their wedding day hung on the wall next to where Rachel sat.

"I like it," she said as he placed a mug of strong coffee on the table. His mug contained a red liquid. Checking his right hand, Rachel smiled.

Picking up on her attention, he said, "You were right, as usual, but don't look so smug about it. I followed your advice and… well, Brenda told me to see the good doctor about the shaking hand. It turned out I was imbibing too much caffeine. As you can see, I've switched to fruit tea, sometimes hot water, and problem solved."

Rachel had picked up on a tremor Waverley was in denial about on her two previous voyages and plucked up the courage last time out to challenge him on it. She was worried it might be Parkinson's disease, or that he was drinking too much alcohol. Caffeine overuse was a much better outcome.

As if reading her mind, he said, "At least I can still drink Scotch."

"Well, the fruit tea is suiting you. You look rather well."

"Apart from being a little overweight, I feel better for it. I should have taken Goodridge's lead; he hardly touches caffeine."

He's also teetotal, thought Rachel, but didn't mention it. "Did I ever tell you married life suits you?" She looked at his waistline, which, she had to agree, was bigger than when they had first met, as he'd since married a senior baker, but it appeared to have stopped expanding and was a small price to pay for happiness.

"Yes, you did. I'd say the same for you, but you seem drawn. You'd better tell me why you're here."

Rachel was pleased he had misinterpreted her drawn look, as he described it, as being due to her real reason for visiting his office.

"As I said before, it's probably nothing."

"But?" he quizzed, taking a slurp, which Marjorie would most certainly disapprove of, of tea. She was pleased her friend wasn't here to witness it.

"I was wondering. Do you have a missing passenger?"

Waverley frowned. "What of it?"

"Is it a man called Darrell Baker?"

Waverley almost dropped his mug. "How would you know that?"

"I heard the announcements this morning calling for someone of that name and it didn't take much working out."

The chief visibly relaxed, but Jason was on it. "I get it now. Is this the guy from the restaurant last night? The one I—"

"Met, yes," said Rachel, not wanting Jason to reveal how he had almost punched the man's friend.

Waverley interrupted. "You met the man who went missing, Rachel. Why does that fill me with dread?"

"I met him three times, actually; well, twice properly and once when I knocked him out of the way of a fast-moving car," said Rachel. "We had stayed at the same hotel after arriving in Mumbai, but I didn't meet him until yesterday morning. We then encountered him briefly at the O Pedro restaurant last night."

"He was trying to chat her up," explained Jason, his face reddening. "And his mate was making a play for Sarah, sir."

Honesty can sometimes be a flaw, Jason, Rachel thought.

"Ah, so you mean you had a run-in with the fellow? I still don't know why it should concern you, Rachel," Waverley's eyes swivelled in her direction. "Unless... did you say you pushed him out of the way of a moving car? Was he some kind of drunk?"

"No, I don't think so, but now you've confirmed it is him that's missing. The car thing might not have been an isolated incident. I fear something untoward might have happened to him."

"According to his friends, he didn't know anyone in India, so I don't imagine him almost getting run over is relevant. Driving in Mumbai is haphazard and downright dangerous most of the time."

"Except this car mounted a kerb and accelerated towards him. If I hadn't reacted so quickly, he would have been dead or seriously injured."

Waverley rubbed his chin, eyes bulging. "Any thoughts, Goodridge?"

"Rachel's hunches have served us well in the past, sir. But the state Baker was in last night, I'd say our original theory is correct. Sorry, Rachel."

"What's your theory?" Rachel was disappointed Jason wasn't trusting her instinct.

"That the man was so inebriated, he fell asleep or visited a brothel," Waverley couldn't look her in the eye for the last part of the sentence.

"That's usually what happens in these cases," said Jason. "He'll catch up with us in Goa once he wakes up and realises he's missed the sailing. His boss says his behaviour was unusual, so she thinks it's a plausible explanation, and we're inclined to agree."

And very convenient for the cruise line, Rachel stopped herself from snapping. "Maybe," she said. "*If* he wakes up."

Colour drained from Waverley's face. "Look, Rachel. I realise you have a tendency to attract murder and mayhem at work and leisure, but this time I believe you're barking up the wrong tree. Just because you met him – although that's usually reason enough – doesn't mean he's been murdered."

"Has anyone heard from him?"

"Not yet, but it's barely nine-thirty in the morning. From what his friends say, I'd be surprised if he comes round before lunch. At worst, he could have passed out and been robbed. Perhaps someone's nicked his phone. Sadly, it happens." Waverley's eyes pleaded for her to accept his explanation.

"Does that mean you will not investigate his disappearance?"

"There's nothing to investigate, Rachel." It was Jason's turn to sound exasperated. "You saw the man. He could barely stand up when he joined his mates. I'm with the chief on this one. He'll wake up somewhere and realise his mistake. If someone robbed him, he'll find the British embassy and make contact through them. And if he wakes up in someone else's bed, he'll get a train or flight down to Goa and meet the ship there."

"I believe he's American, so I suppose he could go to the US Embassy if he's in trouble," said Rachel, thinking out loud. "Don't you have his nationality on file?" She knew her tone sounded accusatory, but the security team had clearly done little to find the missing man.

"Of course we do, and you're half-right. He's got dual nationality. Whichever embassy he makes his way to – if needed – we'll see him soon," said Waverley, his tone dismissive.

"I'm not so sure you will. And I don't like coincidences. First, he's almost run over, and now he disappears. Darrell's far too ambitious to miss the sailing. I believe he's first in line for a very lucrative promotion. A promotion someone might kill for."

"Really, Rachel? Can't you hear how farfetched this all sounds?" said Waverley.

"I wonder if someone drugged him last night. I don't understand why he'd let himself get so out of control when he wanted to make a good impression on his boss."

"Perhaps he bought drugs. They're easy to get hold of. It happens, Rachel," but Waverley was looking less self-assured.

"He wasn't the only one who had an accident yesterday. A woman called Carol North fell down some steps inside the caves on Elephanta Island. She told us she thought someone pushed her."

"And you just happened to be passing?" Waverley's neck redness was a warning sign he was losing patience.

"We get lots of reports from people with overimaginative minds who visit those caves. Some are really far out," said Jason.

"I see," snapped Rachel. She remembered she herself had been unsure whether Carol had imagined the push, except there had been the shadow. She let that one go for now. The priority was finding Darrell. "What about the friend Darrell was with? Gaz. Have you asked him what happened? They were together when they spoke to us in O Pedro. Even if Gaz was drunk too, I can't see him leaving a friend alone under a table or wherever in the middle of a city like Mumbai."

"Give us some credit, Rachel. We have spoken to a few people from his company. Dr Pearl Pantoni reported him missing after he didn't attend an early morning team-building session in the games room. She contacted her boss, who in turn checked Baker's room before contacting us." Waverley thought for a moment. "What's the woman's name, Goodridge?"

"Dr Tia Stone, sir."

"That's right. Dr Stone spoke to a few of Baker's colleagues. After they left the restaurant, they went on to a nightclub. Apparently, he was so drunk he told them all to clear off – I'm putting that politely, but I'm sure you can imagine what he actually told them to do. Gary Jacobs tried to persuade him to call it a night. When he refused, Jacobs stayed with him for a while, but they got into an argument and Mr Baker threatened him, so Jacobs got a taxi back to the ship. I don't believe there's anything sinister going on here other than a group of young people letting their hair down with one or two of them barely able to recall the events of last night."

Rachel opened her mouth to speak, but Waverley stopped her with a hard stare. "And, while I appreciate that you've helped us in the past, and I respect your instincts, Rachel, you're letting previous experience and a reckless driver cloud your judgement. We have a young man who didn't have any friends in India. He went on a night out with a bunch of work colleagues and drank too much – who knows, maybe they all took drugs. Some of these corporate types are renowned for that sort of thing; I've heard lawyers are the worst. Anyway, somewhere along the way he got lost, and is now sleeping it off somewhere."

Gritting her teeth at Waverley's crass stereotyping of law professionals, Rachel persisted. "Do you know if Darrell left the nightclub and whether he was alone when Gaz left him?"

Waverley shook his head. "As there has been no crime committed on board this ship, this is none of our business. If it turns out to be a missing person case, the Mumbai authorities will deal with it. Now, it's good to see you again, Rachel, but I have work to do, which *does* concern me."

Rachel was being dismissed. She stood, hoping as she left that the chief was right for once. She cast one last pleading look towards Jason, but he avoided eye contact.

"In that case, I'll let you get on with your work, gentlemen."

At least she'd sowed the seed. That was all she could do for now. But if they thought she was going to let this drop, they'd misjudged her.

Chapter 9

Gaz Jacobs, whose surname Waverley had so conveniently revealed, was sitting by the pool. Rachel studied him from the internal balcony of the deck above. She guessed he was around Sarah's height at five foot eight. He had loose curly hair hanging over his eyes, which he had a habit of sweeping away.

Gaz was with four of the others from the pharma group. They alternated between swimming and sunbathing and wore costumes varying from the reveal-all to the conservative. Gaz was too pale to be lounging in the bright sunlight and would roast unless he applied a good, strong sunblock. Rachel remembered how much Sarah and the medical team hated the tropical sea days, which resulted in them seeing passengers suffering from mild sunburn to full-on heatstroke.

It had taken a while to track them down, but she should have guessed where they'd be. Rachel studied the pharma group for half an hour, not detecting any anxiety about their missing colleague. The person taking centre stage was an attractive tall woman with long legs; Rachel had noticed her the day before. The others laughed at her jokes or tried to get her attention, but there was one person not joining in with the laughter: a woman sitting on the fringes. She was about ten years older than all the others except Gaz, who couldn't be much older than mid-twenties. This woman was in her early forties, Rachel surmised. Unlike the leggy leader, who wore a bust-revealing bright pink floral bikini, she had a robe over her bathing suit.

What was it Darrell had said to Rachel the day before? They were on a team-building holiday… and yet Earl Spence had told her this morning the trip was all about Dr Stone choosing a new right-hand person, which confirmed what Bernard had told her after dinner last night.

That thought gave Rachel an idea. She checked her watch. Sarah should be finishing surgery and Dr Bentley would be meeting the head of Rejuvenescence Pharma, Dr Tia Stone. Gaz would have to wait – it didn't look like he was going to leave the group anytime soon anyway, and she wanted to speak to him alone. She assumed they would spend most of the day soaking up the sunshine – team building, or vying for position more like. The superficial way they carried on with no intense conversations that might imply they were worried about their missing colleague didn't impress her.

Rachel reached deck two and strolled the familiar corridor to the medical centre. The door was unlocked, so she went straight through. The waiting room was empty, but happy chattering from senior nurse Gwen Sumner's office told her where the medical team would be.

Gwen was first to see Rachel after she gently tapped on the door.

"Rachel!" She hurried over and pulled her into a hug. "It's good to see you. Come in. We were just having coffee – want some?"

"Yes, please."

Neither Sarah nor Dr Bentley was in the room, but Brigitte, Sarah's friend Bernard and Janet Plover, the junior doctor, were all there.

"Sarah should be back any minute. She's gone to check an elderly passenger's blood pressure, and Graham's visiting a passenger on the VIP floor," said Bernard. "The asthmatic I told you about last night."

Gwen shot Bernard a look of disapproval. "You should know better."

"Sorry, boss. It's just that I treat Rachel like she's one of us. I can't remember how it came up. You know I wouldn't discuss passengers with anyone else."

"Make certain you don't," warned Gwen. "You know my stand on confidentiality."

"Isn't he one of the people from Rejuvenescence Pharma? I heard one of them has gone missing," said Rachel, changing the conversation.

"And I thought you were here to see us," remarked the astute Dr Janet Plover.

Rachel felt her face flush. "I am. You're my favourite team, you know that."

"Hmm," said Janet, not looking convinced.

Rachel sat on the two-seater sofa with coffee in hand. Gwen joined her. What she'd said was true. It was good to see them all. It made her feel at home. Meandering around the passenger areas on her own was enjoyable, but being with friends was better. This was her eleventh cruise, and she had known most of the team since her first sailing. Only Janet Plover was a recent addition. Having met her in both a professional and personal capacity a few times, Rachel felt she knew the Welsh bundle of energy as well as the others.

Bernard gave her a knowing look. "I'm sure you're aware of this already, but the missing guy is your new friend and admirer, Darrell Baker."

All heads shot towards Rachel. "You know him?" Brigitte's forehead creased with concern. As much as she and Rachel got on, the French nurse hated the fact that murder investigations followed wherever Rachel went.

"Okay, Rachel. What's this all about?" Gwen cut in. "Do you know more than we do?"

"Not at all. I'm just concerned something bad's happened to him. Contrary to what Bernard says, I didn't know of his existence before yesterday, and I'd hardly say I *know* him now. Our paths crossed three times, though, and from what I saw, I don't believe he would have missed the sailing. I got the impression his ambition would come first."

"Even before you, Rachel?" Bernard cackled. "Jason wasn't impressed with him or his mate, I can tell you that much. I thought he was going to throw a punch at the guy with him."

Gwen frowned. "That's not like Jason. What did they do?"

"Nothing," said Rachel. "They'd had a bit to drink and tried to hit on me and Sarah. They didn't know we were with Jason and Bernard. Gary was about to chat up Sarah when Jason returned."

"I see," said Gwen, stroking her chin. "Did you see them leave?"

Rachel nodded. "They left with the rest of their colleagues. There was some jostling and arguing before their boss joined them, though."

"That Darrell guy was totally wasted," Bernard added.

"Then his friends shouldn't have left him on his own. Mumbai has its share of criminals, and young tourists are easy prey. Let's hope he shows up unharmed." Gwen finished her coffee before placing her mug down on the table and patting Rachel's arm. "He'll turn up. It won't be the first time a passenger has got drunk or mugged in a foreign city before meeting the ship at the next port."

"That's more or less what Waverley said." Rachel drained her mug, still unconvinced.

"It'll be all right, Rachel," said Bernard, offering her a smile of support.

Dr Bentley's voice dispelled the gathering gloom and he and Sarah entered, along with the woman Rachel had seen a few times, Dr Tia Stone. Following an intimate glance towards Gwen, the chief medical officer's eyes set on Rachel.

"Ah, we have another guest with us. Very good to see you, Rachel."

"Likewise," she returned.

"Team, this is Dr Tia Stone, CEO of Rejuvenescence Pharma, a company specialising in turning back time; isn't that right?" Dr Bentley's humour was wasted on his visitor, who barely cracked a smile.

"We are world leaders in groundbreaking research aimed at rejuvenating ageing cells and have developed an exciting new drug undergoing Phase III clinical trials."

Dr Bentley, always the gentleman, introduced the team one by one to the foot tapping Dr Stone before offering her a coffee. Once she had a drink in her hand, she didn't engage in small talk; rather, the foot tapping got faster. Determined not to let her leave the room without mentioning the missing man, Rachel spoke to Dr Bentley but kept one eye on Tia Stone.

"Is there any news on the whereabouts of Darrell Baker?"

Tia Stone stopped her foot tapping, acknowledging Rachel for the first time.

"Do you know Darrell?"

Dr Bentley and the others watched on as Rachel fixed her eyes on the older woman's.

"We met a few times and were supposed to be getting together for a drink." All true, even if slightly exaggerated.

"He didn't mention knowing anyone on board."

"Are you close, then?" Rachel challenged.

"No… er, he worked for me. I needed his full focus this week on the job at hand." Tia glared at Rachel like she was some distracting bimbo, but Rachel was on to her error in a flash.

"You keep using the past tense. Does that mean something's happened to him?"

"Erm… no. I mean, I don't know, but after last night, he might not be working for the company very much longer."

Nice swerve, thought Rachel.

"There's no news about the missing man yet, Rachel. As you know him, I'll keep you informed if we hear anything," Dr Bentley said, oblivious to the tension.

"Thank you," Rachel replied, noting the pallor on the otherwise stony face of Tia Stone.

"I'm sure you're busy, Graham." Dr Stone touched Dr Bentley's elbow. "Should we have that meeting?"

Dr Bentley flushed. "Er… yes. I've asked our senior nurse, Gwen Sumner, to join us. I hope you don't mind."

The eyes hardened – there was no doubt Tia Stone did mind.

"Whatever you think."

Gwen rose from the sofa. "Shall we go then? We can use clinic room two and let the staff finish their drinks."

Rachel doubted Gwen had known she would be attending the meeting beforehand, but the ever-capable nurse leader gave every impression she had.

"I wouldn't like to cross her," said Bernard as soon as the trio left. "That's a woman who gets what she wants at any cost, I think."

Sarah ignored Bernard's comment, turning to Rachel. "What was that all about?"

Rachel shrugged, smirking. "Just probing," she replied.

"It would appear Rachel thinks there's a sinister reason behind Darrell Baker's disappearance," said Bernard, laughing.

"After that performance, I don't think; I suspect it's a strong possibility, and so does she," said Rachel, inclining her head towards the door Dr Stone had left by.

"You've almost got me convinced," said Janet. "Did you see how hard her face turned when she thought you knew the guy? Good twist, Rachel – although a slight stretching of the facts. If I understood right, you only just met the guy."

Rachel grinned.

"Stone by name, stone by nature," remarked Bernard. "Do you think she was knocking him off, or has knocked him off?" he asked Rachel.

Sarah's eyes widened. "Bernard Guinto! Your grasp of the English language and your innuendos never fail to amaze me. But, my dear friend, she can't have been involved with him. She has to be at least twenty years older than him."

Janet chuckled and shared a look with Rachel.

"And your innocence in the ways of the world, despite being married, Sarah Bradshaw-Goodridge, is truly refreshing," Bernard responded.

Sarah's eyes blazed. "I realise a lot of men go in for younger women, but surely not the other way around? Am I being old-fashioned?"

Rachel put her arm around her friend's shoulder. Sarah had now joined her on the sofa, taking the space left by Gwen.

"And a tad sexist," she said gently. "They could have been having a thing, but I doubt it. If they had, I suspect the smarmy Earl Spence would have known about it, and Darrell would have already had the chop. As for whether Dr Stone had anything to do with his disappearance, again, I doubt it. But… I believe she suspects something has happened to her blue-eyed protégé."

"Doesn't he have green eyes? And you had better be wrong about this for once in your life, Rachel, because there's no way we are having any more murderers on board this vessel. Do you hear me?" Sarah's voice had risen almost to a squeal.

"If anything has happened to him, it's more than likely down to his friends' stupidity for leaving him," said Janet.

"I'm sure you're right," said Rachel, squeezing Sarah's arm. As much as she and Rachel got on, Sarah hated being dragged into murder inquiries… if, indeed, this was murder.

"Who's Earl Spence?" Bernard quizzed.

"A guy I met when jogging this morning. He's here – and I quote – 'to make sure whoever gets the new post doesn't damage the company's reputation.'"

"Well, that's Darrell out of the running then, after last night," said Sarah. "Anyway, I'm glad you're here, Rachel, because I have to cancel lunch. I've got to do Graham's routine passenger visits while these two take the on-calls."

Janet's radio burst into life, followed moments later by Bernard's.

"Code Blue passenger deck fifteen. Repeat, Code Blue passenger deck fifteen."

"Right on cue," said Janet. "See you around, Rachel."

Bernard retrieved the emergency bag and he and Janet hurried out of the medical centre.

"I'm going to get some lunch. I'm meeting friends," said Brigitte, also leaving.

"I hope you're wrong about Darrell Baker," said Sarah to Rachel when they were alone. "But if I'm honest, when I heard his name called this morning and discovered he was missing, I got a sinking feeling in my stomach."

"Yeah, me too," said Rachel. "Did you get the chance to ask Jason what he thought?"

"No. He'd already left for work. He got an early call, which I suppose was related."

"Yeah, he fobbed me off when I went to see Waverley. It was odd; he's usually more open-minded."

"He's been edgy recently."

"About what?"

"I don't know. You know what Jason's like – deep rivers and all that." Sarah shuddered before lightening up. "You went to see Waverley? I bet that went down well."

Rachel grinned. "He was all right until I told him why I was there, then he didn't want to know and retreated into his defensive protect-the-cruise-line shell."

"With your history, you can't blame him."

"I guess not. I just wish they were doing more about Darrell's disappearance, that's all. Anyway, if you're not joining me, I'd better go eat something before I fade away. Are we on for dinner?"

"I'm on call from five, but I'll try to get to the Jazz Bar later."

"Okay, I'll see you there."

Rachel left with myriads of theories going through her brain and a deadweight in her gut.

Chapter 10

After giving herself a good talking to, lunch in the buffet gave Rachel the time she needed to relax and absorb the holiday atmosphere. On previous cruises, she had never intended to get involved in crimes committed on board the ship, but this time her obsession with Darrell Baker's disappearance was more about keeping her mind occupied. She recognised it was a means of deflecting her concern and anger about Carlos.

Rachel forked the last cherry tomato, putting it into her mouth, ready to accept Waverley and the medical team's theory that Darrell may have missed the boat for any number of plausible reasons. If they insisted there was nothing sinister about his going missing, who was she to argue? Resolved to enjoy the cruise, she was determined to focus her senses on the beautiful sounds, sights and cuisine of India.

Rachel finished her meal and left the buffet, stopping to treat herself to an ice cream on the open deck. She spotted Gaz Jacobs munching on a burger alone.

So much for focusing on the cruise, her inner conscience teased when she paused at his table.

"Hello. Didn't we meet yesterday?" she said.

His dark blue eyes had been brooding, but now they were alight. He flicked the hair from his face.

"Oh yeah, you saved my colleague's life. Sorry about what happened at dinner. I'd had a bit too much to drink. I hope we didn't offend you."

"Not at all." Rachel took a seat. "I'm pleased to run into you. I wanted to explain to your friend about Jason seeing you both off like that. I'm sure you meant no harm."

"None at all, but if we were rude, I apologise."

"Where is Darrell, by the way?"

"You know his name... oh yes, I remember him telling me now; you'd met earlier, before the kamikaze car driver fiasco."

"Yes, he bumped into me, then I returned the favour." Rachel tried to make light of her encounters. She looked into Gary's eyes. "Sorry, I can't remember your name?"

"Gary, but most people call me Gaz. You're Rachel, right?"

She smiled. "Right."

Gaz had finished his burger and was staring into a glass of cola. Finally, he looked up.

"Darrell didn't make it back for the sailing. I don't know where he is."

"Oh," said Rachel. "Didn't you return together?"

"Truth is, he was acting weird. None of us know each other that well. We've only met through online meetings and email. He was fine earlier in the evening, but he got kind of funny later. I haven't been with the company that long, but there's been a lot of friction, so the reason for this cruise was to do some team building. At least, that was the pretence."

"Why do you say that?"

"None of us knew the boss and the head of PR would join us for a start. Then yesterday, Stoney – she's the boss – summoned us all together in the hotel and gave us a pep talk about needing to pull our socks up and work better as a team. We got a right lecture about petty arguments and the like. In many ways, she was right. When the boss leaves the meetings, there's a lot of bickering and whatnot, but I try not to get involved in that sort of thing. I just do my job, get a good salary and spend most of my spare time cooking. I'd love to be a chef, but my parents want me to get on and are super proud that I'm working for an expanding company, so I work hard, keep my head down and cook for a hobby."

"I think Darrell might have mentioned the team building. I can see why it would be a surprise having your boss show up. But surely she could have had that conversation with you all without the expense of a cruise to India."

Gaz laughed. "You're right there. My theory is there's more to it than that. Darrell's in line for a big promotion –

at least, that's what he and most of us thought, but it turns out the cruise is now part of the selection criteria. He's annoyed about it, that's for sure, but I think he still would have won, despite Earl – the PR manager – having it in for him. That was until he got smashed last night."

"Earl Spence? I met him this morning when I was jogging," said Rachel.

"I'm impressed," said Gaz, wiping his mouth with a napkin. "Amazing Earl was up so early after a late night."

"You said Darrell was drunk last night. Did he do anything that would have annoyed your boss?" Rachel asked.

"Stoney went back to the ship after we left the restaurant, so she didn't see the worst of it. And yeah, he was totally out of it. That's what's been bothering me."

"What do you mean?"

Gaz looked around as if checking they weren't being overheard. "I'm not sure, really. You see, I was knocking the booze back because I like to let my hair down, you know, and I can usually hold the drink, but the stuff I was drinking was strong. At first, I tagged onto Darrell 'cos I was pretty certain he'd get the promotion and I wanted to be in with him when he did. That way, I could stand a chance of getting his job."

Rachel liked his honesty.

"Turns out, he's easy to talk to. I like him. Some of the team are really full of themselves, you know what I mean?"

Rachel helped Gaz come to the point, feeling her stomach tensing.

"You're wondering why he would drink so much and lose control?" she prompted.

"Yeah. Not only that. As I said, I was knocking the drink back, but I only saw Darrell have one alcoholic drink."

Rachel's eyes widened. "Are you sure about that?"

"Pretty sure. I kept offering to get them in, but he refused."

"Did he buy a drink himself?"

Gaz rubbed his forehead. "I don't know. I was back and forth to the bar with Matt – he's based in Cardiff. Neither of us drink wine, which was all Earl had ordered for the table. Matt was moaning all the time about his asthma or something. Darrell was sticking to bottled water whenever I saw him. Later, I got back to the table and he was drinking a cocktail. I didn't see him order it, but he could have done."

"Or someone else bought it for him."

"Maybe. Anyway, it was soon after that he started acting strange, and it all got a bit embarrassing. The girls were too busy sucking up to Earl, trying to get on his good side, to notice it, but Earl gave him daggers. Darrell got louder and less inhibited. I thought he was going to say or do something stupid. To be honest, I was glad when we joined you and your friend."

"But that didn't work out too well."

"Nope. Then the boss turned up. She and Earl got into a tête-à-tête. At one point, Earl nodded towards Darrell when he was looking spaced. Stoney wasn't taking too much notice. I expect she knows Earl and his ways.

"Soon after that, we all left. Stoney was going back to the ship, so Earl said he'd make sure she got back safe. The rest of us took off to a nightclub recommended by one of the waiters. Earl joined us later.

"It's all a blur after that. I had way too much to drink on the company. From what I can remember, I was fed up with them all; every time I looked around, someone was arguing with someone. Darrell was stumbling around, talking to himself. I thought he might get kicked out at one point. Then when he fell into another geezer's girlfriend. I was scared the guy would land him one; instead, the guy patted him on the back and helped him to a seat."

"Interesting." Rachel wondered what Jason would have done if Darrell and Gaz hadn't left their table as quickly as they did. "So why didn't he come back to the ship with you?"

Gaz shrugged. "It's hard to say."

"You mean remember?"

"Yeah, that."

Rachel was almost certain Waverley had told her Gaz had argued with Darrell and had been told to clear off. Why wasn't he mentioning this?

"Do you remember leaving the nightclub without him?"

"Not really. Lizzie – that's one of the girls – said Darrell told me to get lost. I obviously left at some stage and got to my stateroom okay, but I don't remember how. This morning I woke up with a splitting headache, still wearing my clothes. I feel bad, leaving a mate and him not turning up. I shouldn't have drunk so much. The others are gloating over how he'll never get the promotion now."

"Did any of the others see Darrell leave the nightclub?"

"Not that they're saying. Sangita – she's based in Mumbai – thinks he decided his promotion was toast after he and Earl had words in the nightclub and jumped before he was pushed."

"And what do you think?" Rachel asked.

Gaz shook his head. "I can't see him doing that, but then again, I wouldn't have thought he'd get blotto in front of everyone either. The others had a few drinks and might have been drunk, but they reckon they were all pretty much in control. I was the only one that went overboard, and that all started with Carol giving me a prepaid at the start of the night."

Rachel's ears pricked up. "Who's Carol?" She pretended not to know.

"Some say she's the second favourite for the promotion. Except Lizzie reckons it's unlikely she'll get it 'cos the word is, she's had run-ins with the boss. Probably a woman thing."

Ignoring the sexist reference, Rachel pressed, "Why did Carol give you a prepaid card?"

"Dunno. I assume Earl dished them out and everyone got one."

"Is that usual?"

"The company's very generous with its allowances, so yeah, I guess it could be."

"Would Darrell have been into drugs?"

Gaz thought for a moment. "I don't think so. Even if he was, he didn't know anybody in India apart from Sangita. We only met her two nights ago. Lizzie had arranged a shindig but excluded Darrell and Pearl Pantoni from the invites. She said it was a mistake, but I'm pretty sure it was deliberate. So Darrell didn't meet Sangita until yesterday morning. I don't think they clicked."

"Hm," said Rachel. "Do you think Lizzie and the others also knew about the trip's change of purpose?"

"If they did, they didn't tell me. But we were notified the night we arrived that we had to attend a meeting in the hotel the next morning, which seemed strange."

"Is Pearl a friend of Darrell's?"

"Nah, the others see her as an outsider. She doesn't say a lot, and she's older than the rest of us. By rights, she should be first in line for promotion. She's got a doctorate in pharmacokinetics and has been with the company the longest. Darrell says she doesn't have the drive. Did anyone ever tell you you're easy to talk to, Rachel?"

Rachel could see by the look in the young man's eyes where he wanted to take the conversation next, but she was laser-focused.

"I'd still like to talk to Darrell. Do you have his phone number?"

Gaz sighed but took the rejection with good grace. "It won't do any good. I've been calling him on and off all morning. I'm sure Dr Stone and Pearl have too. It was Pearl who raised the alarm."

"Odd, for someone who wasn't a friend. How did she notice?"

"He didn't show for the first team-building session. She was worried."

"I see. Is his phone switched off?"

"It could be. It goes straight to voicemail. If you let me have your number, I'll text it to you."

Rachel wrote her number down on a piece of paper from her handbag. A few seconds later, she felt her phone vibrate.

"I think your friends are looking for you." Rachel noticed the dark-haired guy and Carol North heading their way.

Gaz turned around to check. "That's Carol and Matt."

"I'll leave you to it, then. Nice talking to you, Gaz."

"Hope to see you around, Rachel," he called after her.

You most certainly will, she thought. *But not in the way you're hoping.*

Chapter 11

"This is a passenger announcement. Could Mrs Jacobi-Prince make her way to reception, please? Mrs Jacobi-Prince, please make your way to the main reception."

Carlos! Rachel felt sick. Not willing to wait for the lift, she took the stairs two at a time down to deck four, where she found a flustered Waverley pacing up and down.

"Is he all right?" Rachel forced the words to sound measured, but her eyes pleaded with the security chief to tell her everything was fine. Sweat dripped from Waverley's forehead. He mopped it away. Rachel could tell by the look on his face something was seriously wrong. Her heart felt like it would explode any minute.

Passengers' heads turned their way. "Just tell me," she snapped.

Waverley cleared his throat. "Let's go to my office. It's quieter there."

Just as they left the main atrium, Sarah came hurtling round a bend, almost bumping into Waverley.

"What's happened? Is he okay?" She echoed what Rachel had already asked.

Waverley's forehead creased, but he said nothing. Rather, he marched down the nearest stairs towards deck three. Sarah took Rachel's hand as they hurried after him.

"I heard the call. What's happened?"

"I don't know, he hasn't told me." Rachel was struggling to maintain control; her mouth felt like sawdust and she was resisting the urge to pass out. She inhaled and exhaled deep breaths, willing Waverley's heels to move faster. Too many times, as a detective, Rachel had been the bearer of bad news and she'd witnessed every reaction possible. She was determined to stay in control.

Sarah had a tight grip on Rachel's hand. Waverley took an eternity to unlock his office door. Sarah hurried inside, almost falling over him in her rush, while Rachel marched forward.

"Coffee?" he asked.

"Never mind about coffee. Where is he? What's happened?" Rachel implored, unable to bear the tension a second longer.

"I'm so sorry, Rachel, he's dead."

Rachel collapsed onto Waverley's sofa. Sarah sat next to her, pulling her into a hug.

"What happened?" Rachel's voice didn't sound like her own. It had a quiet squeak, barely recognisable.

Waverley's face mirrored their concern. "A shopkeeper found him early this morning down a back alley."

Rachel scrunched her eyes tightly closed. *Why did I let him go? I should have stopped him.* Picturing the love of her life dead in some Chinese back alley was unbearable.

"Was he murdered?" She forced her eyes open.

"It's uncertain, but that's what it looks like. I was about to lecture you on always being right, but I did not know you cared about the man so much. You told me you had only just met."

Waverley's eyes filled with compassion. Sarah and Rachel stared at the chief, then at each other, before both bursting into hysterical laughter. Relief replaced terror as they hugged each other while the baffled chief of security watched on.

Finally, Rachel looked up at Waverley. "You're talking about Darrell Baker?"

Waverley's concern turned into a frown. "Yes, of course. Who else would I be talking about?"

Rachel couldn't speak.

"Carlos," Sarah offered. "We thought you were talking about Carlos."

Realisation dawned on Waverley's face. "Oh, my goodness! I'm so sorry, Rachel. If I'd thought the announcement would cause you personal alarm, I wouldn't have put it out. Sometimes I forget you have a family too. Although I'm confused as to why you believed someone would murder Carlos in Mumbai."

"You didn't mention Mumbai," said Sarah.

"Didn't I?"

"No," said Rachel, exhaling. "I thought you were talking about Wuhan."

"Carlos is in Wuhan?" Sarah asked. "The city in China where that new virus has been discovered? Now I see why you're so worried."

"Can someone please explain to me what the hell is going on?" Waverley snapped.

"I can't say any more," said Rachel. "But I will have that coffee now, please."

Huffing and puffing, Waverley called down to the kitchen and took his exasperation out on the poor person at the other end of the phone. Sarah raised quizzical eyebrows, but Rachel shook her head. Now was not the time to discuss this.

Waverley took a few telephone calls while they waited for the drinks to arrive, which gave Rachel time to calm her frazzled nerves. Once their coffees were on the table, along with a fruit tea for the chief, he looked unsure whether to proceed.

"So what happened to poor Mr Baker?" Sarah asked.

"They found him in a back alley. I'm awaiting a report from the pathologist in Mumbai, but the police believe his death is suspicious. There was a nasty blow to the side of his head. A fall could have caused it, but we won't know until later. Also, he seems to have another mark the police are not sure about."

Sarah's nose wrinkled with disgust. "Another suspicious death?"

"Would the blow or blows have killed him?" Rachel asked.

"We'll have to wait on the autopsy report. The police captain says he either stumbled from drink and hit his head or someone took him by surprise. There's no evidence of a fight, but the pathologist will tell us more once he or she has had the chance to examine the body."

"That's awful either way," said Sarah.

"I doubt he would have been able to defend himself if someone attacked him," said Rachel.

"What do you mean?" Waverley asked.

"Before you called me just now..." Sarah clasped Rachel's hand again, "...I had been talking to Gaz Jacobs. He's convinced Darrell hardly had anything to drink last night—"

"But when we saw him, he was pretty drunk," Sarah interjected.

"Precisely. Gaz's story makes my theory someone might have drugged him more plausible." Rachel challenged Waverley with her eyes.

"If he took drugs, he may well have done so of his own free will," Waverley snapped.

"I don't believe he would do that, not when he was trying to impress his boss. If someone drugged him while he was still in the restaurant, it would explain the inappropriate behaviour in front of Dr Stone."

"And the same person who drugged him could have followed him when he left the nightclub, and later robbed him," finished Sarah.

"You're getting good at this," Rachel found herself laughing again.

Sarah blushed. "I've obviously spent too much time with you."

"Hey! Don't blame me. You're the one married to a security officer."

"Could we get back to the point?" said Waverley. "If what you're saying is true, then our killer needn't be on board this ship. They could have been targeting tourists."

"I can't see it being a local. It's much more likely to be one of his colleagues," said Rachel.

"Why can't it just be a plain and simple mugging?" Sarah asked. "You agreed with my theory. Anyone could have drugged him and followed him to and from the nightclub."

"It's a possibility," Rachel conceded.

"Before you continue with your wild accusations about it being one of his colleagues, you should also know his wallet was missing," said Waverley.

"Because the killer wanted to make it look like someone had robbed him," Rachel countered.

Waverley sighed heavily. "Rachel, I wish for once you had been wrong about something happening to him. But it's still more than likely an opportunistic robbery. The mugger may not have intended to murder him."

"What are the police suggesting other than suspicious death?" Sarah asked.

"They are being open-minded, although one theory is like Rachel's. We have to admit the killer could be with us, but crimes like this are not uncommon against tourists in Mumbai. The Mumbai police will keep us informed of any developments once the post mortem has concluded and they have examined CCTV footage from the nightclub. In the meantime, they have informed the US Embassy and his next of kin."

"What have they suggested you do?" Rachel asked.

"Nothing for now. The crime was committed on Indian soil and comes under their jurisdiction. If they discover anything that suggests someone on board is responsible, the inspector says they will ask the Goan police to board the ship tomorrow. He suggested they might do that anyway, depending on cooperation, to interview the dead man's colleagues about his last movements and to ask whether any of them saw anything suspicious. I don't think there's any need to mention you meeting him in the restaurant. It doesn't seem relevant. The accident or murder took place after he left the nightclub, which was much later."

"From what Gaz told me, though, the initial doping took place in the restaurant. That's one reason I don't believe it's a random killing."

"He could have been a drug user, Rachel, or your new friend Gaz might be mistaken." Waverley seemed confident for the first time since Rachel had received the awful summons.

"Surely you're going to do some preliminary investigations. I can help with that," said Rachel.

Waverley eyed her carefully. "I forbid it. You are not to go around interviewing VIP guests, Rachel. Back me up, Sarah."

Sarah chuckled. "I'd love to, Chief, but she doesn't listen to me on such matters. I wouldn't waste my breath."

"Look, I've already got to know Gaz a little. He's open and honest. It won't be my fault if I bump into him again. Sarah and I also met Carol North yesterday when she took a tumble down those steps – something I mentioned to you this morning, if you remember. And I've met Earl Spence, the head of PR."

Waverley grimaced. "My, my. You have been busy."

"And Rachel and I met Dr Tia Stone at lunchtime," said Sarah. "In fact, Bernard and I had to extricate poor Graham from her clutches, or she would have still been with him. She's wangled an invitation to the officers' dining room for dinner this evening. I think, under the circumstances, I should invite Rachel."

"Okay. I concede it might be useful for you to do a little surreptitious digging," said Waverley. "As long as you report back to me or Jason."

"Deal," said Rachel, feeling considerably brighter now she had something to occupy her mind.

Waverley cleared his throat again. "Erm, Rachel. Are you sure you're up to this with this Carlos thing going on?"

"Carlos is fine. The announcement was a shock, that's all."

Waverley held his palms up. "You don't want to talk about it. I understand. I was in the navy, remember? But do be careful. It's easy to let your guard slip when you're worrying about something else."

"Thank you. I won't do anything stupid." But an inner voice told her that before the investigation was over, she was highly likely to do just that.

Chapter 12

After the meeting with Waverley, Rachel and Sarah went to one of their favourite venues. Creams was a patisserie with a surcharge where they could usually find a quiet spot to chat.

"I thought you were working this afternoon," said Rachel.

"I am, but it didn't take long to do the first few visits. Two of the other passengers weren't in their rooms, so I left a note under their doors and went back to base. That's when Bernard and I rescued Graham from Tia Stone's clutches. I don't like saying it, but I can't warm to her at all."

Rachel thought back to the few occasions she had observed the CEO the day before and to how Dr Stone behaved in the nurses' staffroom at lunchtime.

"I guess you need to be single-minded to build a company from scratch the way she has. I wonder how she copes with having a board to answer to."

"I can't imagine her answering to anyone," said Sarah.

"Mm, I know what you mean. I got the impression Dr Bentley took Gwen along for protection once Dr Stone opted to do the flirting thing."

"He did, but when they came out of the meeting, Gwen had to go to a procurement meeting with managers from other departments."

"Poor Gwen."

"Poor Graham more like. We could see he was struggling to shake the Stone woman off, so we went to his rescue."

"And how did 'the Stone woman' take it?"

"Miffed, but she still wangled herself an invitation to the officers' mess for dinner. Graham made it clear after she'd gone that we all needed to be there and thanked us for our help. Bernard teased him about it, but he wasn't seeing the funny side. Having said that, the company's portfolio impressed him, the novel drug in particular."

"Did he say what this drug does? Earl Spence implied it rejuvenates ageing cells."

"I didn't get the chance to ask him about it. I heard the passenger announcement, excused myself and flew upstairs. We'll find out more over dinner if it's not a big secret. Graham won't mind you coming along. I'm sure he'll be pleased to have another ally."

Rachel felt herself relax. "He may mind if he realises there's a dead body involved," she said, laughing.

A waiter interrupted the conversation, and they ordered lattes and cinnamon swirls, something they both enjoyed.

"Graham will have been told about the discovery, so as long as no other bodies show up, he'll be philosophical about it. Do you really believe one of Darrell's co-workers killed him?"

Rachel paused for a moment, checking their surroundings. Creams was relatively quiet apart from a large party close to the entrance who were devouring a traditional afternoon tea with sandwiches, cakes and scones loaded on a tiered cake stand. A huge chocolate cake caught her eye as their waiter returned with their drinks and swirls.

"I think I've changed my mind," Rachel said after he left. "Have you seen that cake?"

Sarah turned her head after cutting her swirl in half. "They do wonderful treats in here, don't they? I avoid the place when you're not with me, otherwise I'd be on a permanent sugar rush. Now, are you going to answer my question or drool over that chocolate cake?"

"You can't blame a girl for looking." Rachel grinned, then became more serious. "Back to your question, though. Yes, the odds of it being one of them are higher than it being a random stranger. I don't believe Dr Stone had anything to do with it, but she seemed rattled by Darrell's disappearance, which makes me think she could be hiding something. Unless she feels guilty for putting them under so much pressure that one of them might have done something criminal."

"I expect she'll feel even worse when she hears Darrell's been found dead."

"Serves her right for telling them they were going to have a team-building holiday, and then showing up out of the blue to make it a competition."

"What kind of boss would do that?"

"Her kind," said Rachel, taking a sip of her latte. "Mm, this is so good. You know, it wouldn't surprise me if it was more Earl Spence's decision to spoil the holiday fun. I wonder if he expressed misgivings about her first choice. From what Gaz says, everyone had thought it was in the bag for Darrell."

"Until they got to Mumbai, you mean?" Sarah asked.

"Yep. That's when the knives came out—"

"Or the blunt instruments."

"Ha, ha. Funny, Sarah. You rarely joke about such things. Is this Jason's influence?"

"Not really. More like Bernard's."

Rachel smiled. She could imagine Bernard joking in exactly the same way as Sarah had just done. He had a wicked sense of humour and could tease without mercy.

"What are you smiling about?"

"I was just imagining Bernard saying something like that to Brigitte and picturing the reaction."

Sarah laughed. "Brigitte won't be happy about the latest development, full stop. But like Graham, as long as there are no bodies on board the *Coral*, she'll pretend it didn't happen." Her friend's tone turned serious. "Are you okay now, Rachel? That was a terrible shock when we both thought the call was about Carlos."

Rachel felt her stomach churn. "Waverley can be so thoughtless."

"I guess he thinks you have a sixth sense, seeing as we always go on about your gut feelings. He would never have put the call out if he'd realised where Carlos was."

Rachel frowned, watching the tea party group laughing while munching on slices of chocolate cake.

"I suppose not," she muttered.

"While we're on that subject, isn't it time you told me what he's doing and why he's in a city where the new SARS virus has appeared?"

Rachel bit into her cinnamon swirl and considered whether she should tell Sarah what was happening. What if it slipped out to Jason, and he mentioned it to someone else? Carlos would be in danger.

She made her decision. "Sarah, you know I would trust you with my life, but this is not my life. It's Carlos's. Promise me you won't say anything to anyone other than Jason. I don't want to make you keep secrets from your husband."

"What about Waverley? He already knows where Carlos is."

Rachel weighed that knowledge up. "He's also already made it clear, as a navy bod, he knows about confidentiality. Jason was in the army, so you can tell him as long as you impress upon him the need for secrecy."

Sarah nodded. "Okay."

"What do you know about the new virus?"

"Just what Graham's been told via the World Health Organisation; that there's an outbreak of a novel coronavirus in Wuhan City, China."

Rachel checked the surrounding area once more before saying, "I can't say too much, but do you remember how, when we were on honeymoon, I discovered Carlos had been in the Italian special forces?"

"How could I forget?"

"And that he'd been involved in Anglo-Italian missions in the Middle East?"

"Yes, I remember. I also remember the Italian woman he'd worked with. The one we nicknamed Aphrodite."

Rachel forced a grin. "A week before Christmas, someone from the UK's Secret Intelligence Service, MI6, contacted Carlos, sounding him out over a joint mission with the Italian equivalent, which might mean a visit to China in the near future. It seemed there'd been some chatter concerning something that might become a matter of national security."

Sarah's jaw dropped as her eyes widened. "And MI6 don't have enough spies of their own?"

"I was just as incredulous when Carlos told me about the contact. Apparently, the Chinese are well versed on British spies and vice versa. MI6 needed someone out of the normal loop."

"That's ridiculous – putting civilians at risk like that." Sarah's nose flared and she sucked her lips, something she'd always done when stressed.

"Believe me, I was just as angry and bewildered about it all, but at the time it seemed like it was just murmurings. They were sounding out a few possibilities for a last-minute trip if required. Carlos said he wouldn't go if I didn't want him to."

"Which made you feel guilty. Why do men do that?"

Rachel sighed heavily. "You're right. But when I thought about how I put my life at risk every single day, and how he rarely complains about my working hours, I caved. Whether I would have done so if I wasn't so preoccupied with catching a serial killer at the time is another matter."

Sarah scrunched her nose. "Oh, Rachel, I worry about you and your job at times. Don't you think it's time to consider a career change?"

"What? As a security officer on board a cruise ship?" Rachel laughed. "To be honest, when Captain Jenson mentioned on the last cruise there would be jobs for both me and Carlos if we wanted them, I was sorely tempted. If I'd known then I'd be in this position, I'd have snapped his hand off. But going back to the matter in hand, I assumed nothing would come of it. Carlos told me he used to get these approaches all the time before he met me and they rarely came to anything."

"But the approach became a mission?" Sarah sounded glum.

Rachel reached for her forearm. "Worse. It became a joint mission with his old partner from Italy. He's been gone for ten days."

"Have you heard from him?"

"No contact allowed. He's out there with his Italian wife." Rachel watched for Sarah's reaction.

Sarah's jaw almost hit the table this time. "With Helena AKA Aphrodite?"

"They are Italian tourists on holiday. Please don't suggest they will be anything but professional, Sarah. I really couldn't deal with that thought while knowing they're both in danger."

Sarah's eyes oozed compassion and sympathy, making Rachel's sting.

"Carlos loves you, Rachel. I don't believe for one minute he'd be unfaithful. It's hardly the environment for a fling. But what is it they are doing out there? Don't tell me we're thinking this virus is some sort of biological warfare gone wrong."

"Very astute. I doubt it, but they are scouting around a laboratory in the vicinity of where this outbreak started. The lab's been on the Italian radar for some time. It appears they might be involved in producing and experimenting with new viruses."

The implications of what Rachel had just said clearly hit Sarah full on. Her friend lowered her voice.

"You think the new coronavirus is linked to this lab?"

"I don't think anything, but the joint governments are worried enough to send Carlos and Helena out there to investigate the possibility. If she weren't so beautiful, I'd be pleased she's with him. She saved his life once." Rachel stared into space for a moment. "I just want them to do what they have to do and get out of there. I don't want either of them picking up this new virus; the Chinese are saying it isn't dangerous, but it clearly is. Not to mention I'm not sure what the Chinese authorities do to spies, but I'm pretty certain it wouldn't be pleasant."

"Don't go there, Rachel. Carlos is sensible. I assume their respective governments have an escape plan for them if things go wrong?"

"Yes. But I have no idea what it is." Rachel felt her heart pounding in her chest, not for the first time today. "Now you know everything I do, would you mind if we change the subject?"

"Not at all," said Sarah. "I'll even support you in the Darrell Baker investigation if it helps keep your mind occupied."

"Now you're talking," said Rachel, thoughts still far away.

Chapter 13

"They really didn't like him, did they?" Jack Waverley and Jason Goodridge had spent hours trawling through CCTV footage from the nightclub. This was where the pharma party had spent the evening after leaving the O Pedro restaurant in which Goodridge had come across Darrell Baker and Gary Jacobs. Waverley sensed there was unfinished business and pent-up resentment eating at his favourite officer, who was unusually tense.

They had watched and rewound clips of members of the party arguing with the deceased man that were caught on camera. None of the petty spats appeared to get out of hand as far as Waverley could see. Nothing that suggested any of them might go on to commit murder.

Goodridge remained straight-faced. "Professional jealousy, if you ask me – they're all would-be kings and queens. Just a bunch of yuppies."

"Now there's a term I haven't heard for a long time." Waverley grinned. "By that, you mean ambitious young people obsessed with success?"

"Yeah. Young, upwardly mobile professionals." Goodridge scowled, clearly not enamoured with the menagerie of determined wannabes. Waverley's attempt at lightening up his usually chipper officer's mood hadn't worked.

"I knew what you meant, Goodridge; I just didn't know it was a term used nowadays, that's all. It was coined in the 1980s. I'd say that was before you were born."

"Some of our sergeants in the army tormented the middle-class junior recruits with the term. There was one lah-di-dah bloke who got several ear bashings. You know how it could be."

"Indeed. I can't say the navy always treated sailors that well, either, but let's not go down that road. Whatever these people are or are not, they're openly hostile towards our victim, but nothing strikes me as being more than silly bickering."

"They're not that friendly to each other either, sir. They seem to be constantly squabbling. I suspect there's a bitter rivalry between the brown-haired woman and the Asian woman from their body language around each other."

"I noticed that too. Now they are…" Waverley pulled up passenger files on his computer "…Carol North – isn't she the one Rachel said took a tumble?" Not waiting for a reply, he continued, "And Sangita Regum. They completely ignore Dr Pantoni, who reported Baker missing to Dr Stone, don't they?"

"Yeah, she's definitely the outsider. I can't say I like the way the blonde woman and Regum woman throw themselves at the old guy, Earl Spence, either."

"Presumably he's the one who can help further their careers, or perhaps they like older men. The blonde lady is Lizzie Meeton, according to my records," said Waverley.

"They should know better. He's married with two grownup kids, from what I read. Men like that are only interested in one thing. What is fascinating, and slightly odd, is that most of them go outside of the club on their own after Baker leaves."

"Yes, I noticed."

"Doesn't that seem strange? They are in a foreign country, supposedly all together for a night out, and each one of them pops out for some alone time at some stage during the early hours."

"Are you implying they might be buying drugs or something?"

"It's hard to say, sir, but why go out at all if that's the case? Drug sellers would have been roaming the club seeking prospective buyers."

"Not if the proprietor is onto them and wants a clean club."

Goodridge looked thoughtful. "Yeah. That could explain it. I just think the timing's odd when they all go out within an hour of Baker leaving but, unlike him, they come back."

Waverley wondered whether this was significant. "You're suggesting that any of them could have followed him out and done the deed before returning to the nightclub? At least it gives us somewhere to start. We need to find out what they were all doing during their time both inside and outside the club."

"It also brings into question Gaz Jacobs's story that Baker wouldn't leave when he asked him to and that he left without him." Goodridge rewound the footage and they watched the point at which Darrell Baker left, accompanied by Gary Jacobs. Jacobs staggered back inside about fifteen minutes later.

"Good point. Someone's lying here, but is it because they are deliberately trying to misdirect us or they don't remember? Jacobs looks as if he wouldn't remember his own mother's name, let alone what occurred between him and Baker or when the other man left."

"So why say that Baker told him to get lost when, in fact, he left with him? And why did Jacobs return to the nightclub when he told us he got a taxi back to the ship? He's got to be our prime suspect, if we need one."

Waverley hoped Goodridge wasn't letting his brief encounter with the two men the night before cloud his judgement. His body language wasn't encouraging. Every time he cast eyes on the video clips of Gary Jacobs, his fists clenched. It wasn't like Goodridge to lose perspective, but he was a relative newlywed and had been burned in the past when his former fiancée left him for another man.

"From what we've gathered so far, Jacobs isn't in the running for the promotion, so there's no motive. Maybe they went outside and that's when Baker told him to clear off. He was just too drunk to get his facts straight."

Goodridge shook his head. "I'm not so sure. There could be another motive, or perhaps he's not a guy who likes to be told he's not wanted, so he threw a punch."

Now they were getting onto sticky ground. "How did he take it when you told him to leave Sarah and Rachel alone?" Waverley knew Goodridge to be a fair man, but jealousy caused people to do things that were out of character. He needed to quash any lingering animosity.

Goodridge's jaw tensed, before he said, "He seemed to get the message."

"Without argument?"

"There wasn't time. Baker pulled him away, apologising."

"We'll need to interview all of them on their recollections of last night, and that includes Earl Spence. Dr Stone wasn't there, so at least we can rule her out of it. Did your friend get us any CCTV from the restaurant?" Goodridge had called in a favour from an old army buddy who worked for a private security firm in Mumbai. That's how they'd managed to watch the video from the nightclub.

"I didn't ask. Do you think it might help?"

"Who knows? It can't do any harm. We might see something starting up earlier that carried over into the nightclub. Rachel thinks Baker might have been drugged in the restaurant, so it's worth a shot."

"Okay, I'll call her."

"And at the same time, ask if she's managed to find any security cameras outside the nightclub, particularly from the alleyway where Mr Baker was found."

"She's already on that. Some shops have cameras, but they don't all work. Most are just dummies used as a deterrent. Just one question, sir."

"Yes?"

"If the Mumbai police aren't certain it was someone from the ship who attacked the man, and they might send officers on board in the morning, shouldn't we leave any interviewing to them? We've still got a string of thefts to investigate among the world cruisers, and there's the assault claim from last night, not to mention the constant alcohol-related issues."

"I'm well aware of what's going on, Goodridge. Why don't you focus on the assault and I'll get Inglis to help me with the interviews. If Rachel's right, I want to sort this out sooner rather than later. It won't do us any favours having uniformed officers trawling around the ship. The company won't like it."

Waverley had to constantly balance the ship and therefore the cruise line's reputation with the need for justice. He was not one to underreport criminal activity, but he did like to bring every crime to a swift conclusion. Not only for the company's sake but because he genuinely cared about crew and passenger safety. Now they had the pathologist's confirmation that Darrell Baker had been murdered following two blows to the head, the second most likely causing haemorrhaging to the brain, Waverley had to consider the possibility that a passenger was responsible for the murder while the Mumbai police checked out the local angle. Any delay on his part would be unforgivable as well as negligent. Although they were currently sailing under the country of convenience flag, as soon as they docked in the morning, they would be obliged to defer to Indian law.

"Rachel's doing some digging," Waverley added. "She might come up with something."

"She usually does." Goodridge smiled for the first time since they had watched the video footage. "Sorry if I was out of line just now, sir. I don't know what got into me. Must be the heat."

"Don't mention it. You get on with contacting your friend in Mumbai, and then interview the alleged perpetrator of the assault case again. What's his name – Maku? I understand he's denied attacking the woman, and she's dropped the accusation. I don't like domestics on board, Goodridge. Find out if he's coerced her into letting him off. Interview their friends and see if there's been anything like this before. If there's any substance behind the initial allegation, I want him off ship first thing tomorrow morning."

"What if she decides to go with him?"

"Then she's a fool. Are they married?"

"No, sir. One of those onboard get-togethers between staff."

"At least that's something. Perhaps you can convince her she's better off – and safer – without him."

"I'll give it my best shot. From what Dr Bentley says of her injuries, they're consistent with her initial claim. I suspect we'll be one engineer short by the morning."

"Let me know later and I'll give the agency a call. That'll give them time to get someone lined up to take his place tomorrow. And if you decide he attacked the lady, make sure he's confined to an empty cabin, or put him in the brig. I don't want him going anywhere near her before we get rid of him."

"Right, sir. I'll call Rosa, and then I'll deal with our Mr Maku."

After Jason left, Waverley called down for a flask of hot water and a fresh batch of fruit teas before watching the CCTV reel again.

Chapter 14

Sarah had left Rachel to see if she could track down the missing guests and finish her visits. Gaz was lounging by the outdoor pool. Rachel recognised the woman with him as the one he had told her had been excluded from the team's shindig, along with Darrell: Dr Pearl Pantoni, who sat beside an empty sun lounger, still wrapped in a towel robe. Sangita Regum was doing breaststroke lengths up and down the pool. None of the others were with the duo.

"Hi, Rachel!" Gaz called out when she passed by, pretending to be looking for somewhere to sit.

"Oh, hello, Gaz. It's busy out here, isn't it?"

"You can have this bed if you like." Gaz motioned to a sun bed next to his and quickly removed a towel.

"Are you sure it's free?" Rachel asked.

Gaz smirked. "It is now. Matt won't mind. He'll be gone for ages. He's getting something to eat and he likes his food." Rachel noticed a smattering of freckles around

Gaz's nose, brought out by the sun. His cheeks were glowing.

Rachel placed her own towel on the vacant bed while smiling at Pearl Pantoni. "Hello," she said.

"Hi." The answer was glum.

"Are you in the same group as Gaz and Darrell?"

The woman's head shot in Rachel's direction. She looked Italian, except her worried eyes were almost navy blue.

"I am. How do you know Darrell?"

Gaz seemed happy to listen in, so Rachel sat on the bed and turned her head towards the quiet woman. "I met him yesterday at a hotel in Mumbai, and ever since, I keep bumping into Gaz here." She gave a short laugh. "I'm Rachel. Pleased to meet you." She held out her hand.

"Pearl Pantoni."

"Is Pantoni an Italian surname?" Rachel felt the friendly approach was the way to go in this instance. Pearl wasn't outgoing like Gaz.

"It is. My father's half Italian, so I guess I'm a quarter, but I was born in north London. I live and work in Stratford, East London." The clipped tones sounded almost as though she were reciting a CV.

Rachel followed up on the opening. "I know Stratford. I lived in London for a while. My husband's Italian, but he was raised in London. We live in Leicester now."

"You're *married*?" Pearl emphasised the word pointedly in the direction of Gaz, who just shrugged. "Is your husband with you?"

"Not this time. He's working. My best friend works on board along with her husband, so I'm catching up with them."

Gaz's interest was piqued. "Wasn't the Chinese guy you were with in the restaurant last night your husband?"

"No. Bernard's a nurse who works with my friend. He's from the Philippines, not China. Jason, the other guy you met," she grinned, "is married to my best friend, also a nurse on board."

Pearl looked confused. "When was this? I didn't see you last night."

"Darrell and I made a play for Rachel and her friend in the O Pedro, but two men saw us off. Well, one strapping geezer who you wouldn't want to mess with did anyway. The guy called Jason," Gaz explained.

Pearl broke into a grin. "Serves you right. Although I'm surprised you remember," she said. Turning to Rachel, she explained, "Did he tell you Darrell's missing? We think he might have got into trouble in Mumbai, or been robbed. He shouldn't have gone off on his own, and his so-called friend shouldn't have let him."

It was interesting the pharma group hadn't heard that Darrell had been found dead. Waverley was obviously playing the waiting game.

"Gaz mentioned it earlier. It's a shame, I expect you're all worried—"

"It wasn't my fault." Gaz interrupted Rachel. Pearl's pointed remark clearly hadn't been lost on him. "I told you: he didn't want me around. He got himself in a right paddy.

I tried to reason with him, and I honestly thought he was in a taxi on his way back to the ship. Although, to be honest, I can't remember much about any of it. Sangita and Lizzie sort of filled me in on the details."

Pearl didn't seem convinced. "As if either of them cares. But some of us are worried," she said.

"Gaz says Darrell went missing after leaving the nightclub," said Rachel. "Did you see him leave?"

"No. I was in the ladies escaping the noise and the belittling from my colleagues. Those places are not my thing, but it was all part of the show."

"Gaz explained about the team building and the competition for a promotion."

"Did he now?" Pearl shot a scathing look at Gaz.

"What do you all do?" Rachel changed tactic. "I know you work for a pharmaceutical company, but I don't know what that involves."

"Most of us – apart from Gaz here – are senior research scientists. He's an RS but not yet senior. We manage various aspects of clinical drugs trials in hospitals and in the community. We're an expanding company and each of us is based in a different part of the world. You probably know already that Darrell's in New York and Gaz here is in Dublin, where our head office is. Sangita, the one in the pool, is fairly new, and works in a new arm opened in Mumbai. She's from an extremely wealthy family and already thinks she runs the place—"

"Yeah, and don't we know it?" Gaz interrupted. "Matt – like I told you earlier, Rachel – is in Cardiff, and Carol's in the Belfast office."

"And Lizzie, the flirt over there…" Pearl inclined her head to where the long-legged woman wearing the 'almost' bikini was sitting in a jacuzzi surrounded by a group of young men, "…is based in Brussels."

"You really are a multinational conglomeration," said Rachel.

"Did you see the older guy with us last night?" asked Gaz. "Oh, I forgot. You said you met him jogging. Anyway, he's our head of PR: a Texan, based in Toronto. The SRS from there was supposed to be here but handed his resignation in a week before the trip. I don't blame him. I wouldn't want to be in the same place as Earl Spence."

"Me neither," said Pearl. "Did you say Earl was out jogging?"

"Yes, I met him this morning," said Rachel. "He seemed angry when the announcement calling Darrell to reception was made. Perhaps he was worried."

"I doubt that," said Gaz. "More like looking for another reason to stick the boot in. As I said before, he doesn't like Darrell, but until last night and this morning, I thought Stoney would still give him the job."

Pearl's eyes hardened at the mention of Dr Stone. "Don't let her hear you calling her that, or you'll be out of a job. And for your information: if she had decided about who she was going to promote, she wouldn't be ruining our so-called team-building holiday."

"You'd better not let her hear you say that either," Gaz retorted, laughing.

"I met a Dr Stone at lunchtime," said Rachel, "when I went to see my friend in the medical centre. She came in with the senior medical officer. I think they had a meeting."

Pearl shook her head. "She doesn't waste a minute, does she? One of our own is missing, and she's sucking up to the medical director, trying to push drugs." An angry blink of the eye prevented the moisture from becoming tears.

"You like Darrell," Rachel said, feeling empathy for the rather pretty but unassuming woman.

Pearl shook her head aggressively.

"You must," said Gaz. "This is the most I've heard you say since I've known you. Plus, you were the only one concerned enough to go looking for him this morning."

"I didn't expect to like him. He's dismissive and argumentative in meetings. For that reason, I thought he was an overambitious twerp, if I'm truthful. But when we met yesterday – after you all deliberately excluded us from your night out and other stuff – I felt sorry for him."

"That had nowt to do with me," said Gaz. "The girls arranged it. I didn't know you weren't invited."

"And what would you have done if you had known?" Pearl fired back.

Gaz stared at his hands. "Probably nothing. I wouldn't want to cause any more friction. I know what you mean about Darrell, though. We got on really well last night. He was easy to talk to – until he got weird, that is. I think I'd have been made senior if he got the job, but I guess it's going to Carol or Lizzie now."

"Is that why you've been sucking up to them today?"

Gaz's eyes widened. "No, I haven't."

"Liar. I might not say much, but I notice things."

"Okay, so what if I am? I couldn't care less about the job, but me parents do, and I try to keep them happy. I can't see Darrell joining us now. He'll wake up and be on the first flight back to New York."

"That's where you're wrong," said Pearl. "Darrell's not a quitter, so if I were you, I'd hedge my bets."

At that moment, Sangita lifted her head over the side of the pool. "Where's Matt?" she asked, glaring at Rachel.

"Gone to get something to eat," said Gaz.

"What about the others?"

"Lizzie's in the jacuzzi doing what she does best," sniped Pearl. "I don't know where Carol is. Probably off with Earl somewhere."

Pearl might be quiet, but she clearly harboured bitterness against her younger rivals. Perhaps she had been overlooked for promotion once too often. Rachel wondered if that would make her a killer. But she seemed genuinely fond of Darrell, at least from what she'd said. Perhaps they'd shared a joint grudge over the deliberate exclusion.

Sangita leapt out of the pool, soaking them all with spray as she shook water from her long black hair.

"What the..." Pearl complained.

Gaz laughed, winking at Sangita. "Nice try," he said. "But I don't care, it's quite refreshing."

Sangita glowered, before heading towards the jacuzzi.

Rachel hadn't reacted to the drenching, but she felt the show was partly for her benefit. There was an ambitious young woman who had no qualms about who she might tread on to get to the top. Sangita was definitely one to look into. What was it Pearl had said about the wealthy family? There was no doubting the younger woman was used to a life of privilege and most likely indulged. She was also the one who had dismissed the car incident. Rachel's mind pondered on whether Sangita would be ruthless enough to hire someone to drive a car into a rival.

Her musings were interrupted when Matt rushed over, slapping Gaz on the arm. "Stone wants us to meet in the library. Darrell's dead. Where are the others?"

"Jacuzzi," Gaz replied, staring at Matt in open-mouthed astonishment.

Leaving Gaz and Pearl, who he had ignored, to process this news, Matt hurried towards the jacuzzi. Gaz stared at Rachel in disbelief. Pearl's flaming tear-filled eyes glared after the bearer of bad news.

Rachel watched Lizzie and Sangita closely while Matt delivered the news. Their body language suggested they were more inconvenienced than upset by the message. Reluctantly leaving the jacuzzi and the three men they had been laughing and joking with, they collected their robes and belongings from where Pearl and Gaz had hastily departed. Sangita gave Rachel a hard stare, her eyes filled with menace.

"I remember where I've seen you before. You were talking to Darrell at the hotel yesterday. Didn't you also get in the way of a speeding car?"

"Guilty," said Rachel.

"Have you heard the news?" Sangita was almost gloating. "Your new friend Darrell's dead."

"I'm sorry to hear that," said Rachel. "It must be an awful shock."

"Not really."

"Sangie! Come on…" Matt called over his shoulder.

"I'm coming." Sangita swung a white beach bag over her right shoulder and followed the other two inside, leaving Rachel wondering what she'd meant by her last comment.

Chapter 15

The wine bar was quiet when Sarah arrived earlier than expected to meet Rachel for a pre-dinner drink. She had been pleasantly surprised by how quickly evening surgery had gone and, so far, no call outs: a double bonus.

"What can I get you, Nurse Sarah?" Pauline, a member of the wine bar staff, smiled after stifling a yawn. "Sorry, I was up early this morning."

"Don't worry, I understand. Could I have a glass of water while I wait for a friend, please?"

"No problem. I'll be right back."

Sarah scanned the room, observing a couple holding hands and a smattering of holidaymakers around one table. Three of the septet had spent too much time in the sun, she mused. The few people she had seen during evening surgery had been over-roasted adults and a few sunburnt children. All the nurses and doctors had mucked in, which was probably why the evening surgery had seemed quieter than usual, with all the attendees swiftly treated.

Despite numerous announcements during the day, requesting passengers be aware of the dangers of staying too long in the sun and advising them to lather young children with sun cream, some people never listened. Although the nights were a cool seventeen degrees centigrade, the daytime temperatures hovered around thirty-one at this time of year. January was a good time to be sailing India's west coast because it was less humid than summer and there was little chance of rain to ruin holidaymakers' days out. The rainy season in India ran through the British summer months, when the days were hot and humid. Downpours of heavy droplets brought welcome relief, but floods were common. Sarah remembered being caught in a monsoon rain shower not long after she and Jason started dating.

Pauline brought Sarah's water, topped with ice cubes. "If you're waiting for Jason, I saw him earlier with Sonia; she's been through a rough time." Sarah nodded, remembering her husband telling her about the young member of staff who had reported being assaulted by one of the engineering team. "Your man looked like he had the weight of the world on his shoulders."

"I expect he's had a busy day," Sarah said. "But I'm not waiting for him. We're both on call this evening. I'm meeting my friend Rachel. Do you know her?"

Pauline smirked. "No, I haven't had that pleasure, but if she's the one who goes around solving murders, her reputation precedes her."

Sarah sighed, reluctant to mention the recent demise of Darrell Baker, otherwise it would be round the ship faster than a whippet.

"That's the one."

A man was trying to get Pauline's attention at the bar, so she left Sarah to her thoughts.

Jason hadn't been himself of late. She couldn't work out whether it was the stress of his job or adapting to married life that was bothering him. She hoped at some point to ask Rachel about her first year of marriage, in case there were any tips she could give her to help smooth Jason's path. He had been the reluctant – or rather, hesitant – party in terms of commitment.

Rachel had been the same before she'd finally married Carlos, so she might understand what Jason was going through. But it would be hard broaching the subject, knowing Rachel was worried sick about her husband being in China doing undercover work. She must be very secure in her marriage not to be worried about the Italian goddess, Helena, playing wifey.

Sarah felt her lips upturn involuntarily, remembering the unpleasant junior doctor from Rachel's honeymoon voyage. There had been a few not-so-great junior doctors joining the team over the years, so Janet Plover was a breath of fresh air and had fitted right in. Plus, she had a great sense of humour, which was always a bonus.

Recalling Rachel's discovery that her new husband was having clandestine meetings with another woman on their honeymoon, Sarah thought her friend had reacted with amazing restraint. The fact he and Helena had worked together on dangerous missions in the past, rather than he had developed a roaming eye so soon into their marriage, had turned out to be the better of two evils.

Sarah's reminiscences were disturbed when a passenger plonked himself heavily in the seat opposite.

"Hello. Can I get you a drink?" A handsome, though slightly skinny, man with shoulder-length brown hair gazed at her with sparkling brown eyes. She recognised him as one of the Rejuvenescence Pharma group who had been hanging around when Rachel almost killed herself saving Darrell Baker.

"No, thanks. I'm waiting for someone," Sarah replied.

"You work on board, don't you?"

Ten out of ten for observation when I'm in uniform, thought Sarah, but she smiled politely. "Yes, I do."

"What's it like working on a cruise ship?" he asked.

"Why? Are you thinking of applying for a job?" The words were out of Sarah's mouth before she could check them. That must be Brigitte's influence.

"Nah. I've got a good job, thanks. I might even get a promotion sometime soon. I'm Matt, by the way. Are you sure I can't get you a drink while you wait for your friend?" He put a hand up to get Pauline's attention.

Sarah couldn't help warming to the affable Welshman with the open face, but after Jason's reaction to Gaz and

Darrell last night, she didn't want to take any chances of a repeat performance. She shook her head.

"No, thanks. My name's Sarah," she said.

Pauline arrived at the table with pad in hand. "Yes, sir?"

"A bottle of your best Shiraz, please, and one glass," he said, doe-eyed. Sarah chuckled.

Pauline looked at Sarah. "I forgot to congratulate you and Jason on tying the knot."

Matt laughed after Pauline had strolled over to the bar. "That was subtle. Is she a friend of yours?"

"We're all friends on a cruise ship. It's one enormous family."

"Be grateful. It's not like that in the pharmaceutical industry. At least not in our company. They'd stab you in the back as soon as look at you."

Sarah jumped on the cue. "Do you work for Rejuvenescence Pharma?"

"Don't tell me – our CEO is your best mate. That would be just my luck." Matt cackled.

"Not quite, but I have met her."

Matt slapped himself on the head. "Blimey, now I'm in the soup."

"It's all right, I don't know her. I work in the medical centre, and she popped in at lunchtime for a meeting with our chief medical officer."

"Are you a nurse or a doctor?" He strained to look at her name badge. "Ah, a nurse. My sister's a nurse, and my dad. He works in mental health."

"Small world," said Sarah. "Don't tell me – your mum's a doctor?"

"Nah. She's a copper. They don't approve of my career choice at all, but as long as I stay on the research side and don't go peddling drugs, as they call it, they let me off without too much hassle." Matt laughed again, causing himself to wheeze. He pulled out an inhaler, taking two puffs.

This must be the one Bernard saw on boarding day, thought Sarah. "My mum doesn't approve of mine either. Nursing, she doesn't mind, but she hates me working on a cruise ship."

Matt grinned. "I guess she'd rather you and your husband lived next door."

"Something like that," said Sarah, grimacing.

"I take it your husband works on board, or is he on a permanent holiday?"

"He'd like that, I'm sure. His name's Jason, and he works in the security team, so watch yourself."

"No kidding! I met one of that team this afternoon. A big, muscular girl."

"Officer Inglis to you."

"Actually, she told me to call her Rosemary. Nice woman." Matt grinned again. "I didn't meet your husband, though, unless he's late fifties, thinning on top and goes by the name of Weatherly."

Perhaps as well you didn't meet Jason, thought Sarah.

"Waverley," she corrected. "Chief Waverley."

"Oh, was he the boss? That explains a lot. He was far too serious for my liking. My mum's got a great sense of humour, although she sees some horrible stuff. I guess she has to be hard sometimes, and her work can be upsetting. My dad keeps her grounded."

"Her own personal counsellor?"

"Sort of."

"Why were you speaking to a member of the security team?"

"Come on, man… if your fella's in security, you must know."

Sarah returned his grin. "I haven't seen much of him today. I've been too busy treating people with sunburn. Speaking of which, you're looking partly cooked yourself."

Matt shook his head. "It's the fair skin. We don't get much sun in Wales."

"So?" She waited for him to answer her original question.

"Oh, that. One of our lot snuffed it."

Sarah winced at the turn of phrase. "I heard about the death of your colleague. I'm sorry for your loss."

"Yeah, thanks, but we didn't know each other that well, to be honest. Most of us were jealous of the guy because he was in line for a top promotion. Not anymore, though." Matt poured himself a celebratory glass of wine, waving Pauline off from doing it for him.

"Enjoy your wine, sir." Pauline's lips formed a straight line.

"Thank you, Pauline," Sarah called after her, going off Matt by the minute.

"Cheers." He held the glass up, eyes sparkling.

"Even if you were jealous of your colleague, you don't seem very upset about the death of a young man, friend or no friend," Sarah said, glaring.

Matt took a sip of wine, swilling it annoyingly around his mouth before meeting her gaze. "Sorry if that sounded uncaring. Humour's how we deal with things in my family. I didn't mean to be disrespectful. I guess he had people back home in New York who will be heartbroken, but none of them are among his work colleagues. He wasn't popular."

"Because of the imminent promotion, you mean?"

"Mostly that, but he was a moron, to be honest. Intelligent enough but no finesse; no insight into how to treat people."

"Unlike you," Sarah snapped.

"I deserved that. But you didn't know him. He was the type who would tread on his own mother to get to the top, if you know what I mean."

"That's a shame. Did none of his colleagues like him?"

"Nope, except maybe Pearl. Dr Pantoni, that is. I didn't think she cared about him before this trip, but I'd say she'd developed a crush. She was too old for him, mind."

"Is she another manager?"

"Nah. She's the same as the rest of us. We're all seniors in our field except for Gaz. He's fairly new, and a junior. Not sure why he was invited on this trip at all, unless Stone had him in mind for Darrell's job. He seemed to get on all right with Darrell. At least, I thought he did until they argued. And," Matt emphasised, "he was the last person to see Darrell Baker alive, so maybe they didn't get on that much." Matt cackled again.

"Are you suggesting someone might have killed your friend… er, colleague?"

"Good God, I hope not. It was a joke. What I meant was Gaz left him after they argued, and Darrell was falling down drunk. But now you mention it, perhaps that's what security was sniffing around for this afternoon." Matt sat back and wiped his forehead. "Blimey. Don't repeat what I said to your husband. He'll think Gaz did it."

"How did your colleague die?" asked Sarah.

"I didn't ask. I assumed he took drugs or something, or got mugged. Rosemary didn't say exactly, but she asked if any of us took drugs, and if I saw him doing drugs."

"And do you? Did he?"

He smirked. "You're starting to sound like her and my mother. No comment is my answer to that." Matt chuckled before his eyes turned serious. "They wouldn't think any of us had anything to do with Darrell's death, would they? I mean, surely he fell over or something. He was wasted."

"I don't know what anyone thinks," Sarah lied. "I've been at work all day. My husband and I are like ships that pass in the night, if you'll pardon the pun."

Matt's watch buzzed. "Whoops! That's me. We've got a meeting in ten minutes and I said I'd meet Lizzie and Carol beforehand. Nice talking to you, Sarah."

"And you, Matt. I hope you enjoy the rest of your trip."

"I'll try, although it's not a great start, is it? Let's hope no-one else is taken out. You and your friend are welcome to finish the bottle. It's on the company."

Matt sprinted out the door, leaving the almost full bottle of expensive red on the table, and Sarah contemplating what he'd told her.

Chapter 16

As she arrived, Rachel caught a glimpse of Matt's back as he broke into a jog on exiting the wine bar, heading in the opposite direction. Sarah was sitting in one of the side booths.

"You're looking thoughtful. Busy shift?" Rachel leaned down and kissed her friend on the cheek before taking the bench opposite.

"It wasn't bad at all. Everyone helped out, but that's not what I was thinking about. I've just had an interesting conversation with Matt, one of the men from Darrell's group."

"I saw him leave just now. He seemed in a rush. I hope you haven't been upsetting the passengers," Rachel teased.

A waitress appeared, taking an empty wine glass from the edge of the table.

"Would you like two glasses?" she asked.

"Just one for Rachel please, Pauline. I'm on duty, could I have an alcohol-free cocktail?" Turning back to Rachel after the waitress left, Sarah said, "Of course I haven't. Look, he even left wine."

Rachel examined the label. "It looks expensive."

The waitress called Pauline returned with Sarah's cocktail and filled Rachel's wine glass, giving Rachel a knowing look.

"What was that all about?" Rachel asked after she left.

"Your reputation."

"Oh. Does she know about Darrell?"

"No, and don't mention it. Word will spread soon enough, but not from me."

Rachel sipped the strong Shiraz. "Want a taste?"

"Just a sip." Sarah's nose wrinkled.

"He ordered one of the best wines we have and said it was on the company. It appears they get a generous expenses allowance."

"Yes, Gaz told me he was given a prepaid card last night, explaining why he drank too much," said Rachel. "What is it about free food and drink that makes people gorge?"

"I'm not going to answer that."

"I suppose it is like stating the obvious," Rachel conceded.

"That's strong stuff, whatever it is. I prefer white myself," said Sarah, handing the glass back to Rachel and returning to her cocktail.

"But as it's free…" Rachel held her glass up, laughing.

Sarah joined her laughter.

Rachel asked, "So, what did Matt have to say that made you so contemplative? I saw him briefly this afternoon when he appeared at the pool and delivered the bad news like it was a cause for celebration. He had a summons for the bathers to join a meeting with Stoney, as Gaz calls her."

Sarah grinned. "That name suits her. You'll be pleased to hear that, under the circumstances, Graham cried her off dinner in the officers' mess."

"How did she take that?"

"Not well, from what I understand. Graham insisted that, as a sign of respect to her deceased employee, she and the rest of the party might need time to process the news. She didn't dare argue with that."

Rachel could just imagine Dr Bentley's empathetic, authoritative tone dealing with the pushy Dr Stone.

"Is she a PhD doctor or a medical one?"

"She could be either, to be honest. I suspect she has a PhD," said Sarah.

"I met another person with a PhD: Dr Pearl Pantoni. She's a quiet woman with a rather large chip on her shoulder."

"Ah, Matt mentioned her. According to him, she may have had a crush on him."

"Who? Matt?"

"No. Darrell, silly. He also said – and this is the interesting part – that Gaz was the last one to see Darrell alive."

"Mm, that is interesting. Gaz admitted they argued and he left him, but he doesn't remember much about it." Rachel took another sip of wine. "Although I can't see Gaz being a premeditated killer; he's like a puppy. When I asked, he thought Darrell could well have been drugged."

"That explains why Rosemary Inglis was asking Matt whether Darrell, or any of the others, took drugs. Do you believe Gaz?"

"I did, but I suppose he could be lying to cover his tracks. He has no motive, and motive is the only driver when it comes to murder."

"What about means and opportunity? See, I'm learning." Sarah giggled.

"They're important, but not as important as motive. We can all manufacture means and opportunity, but unless there's a motive, we wouldn't need either. Anyway, back to Gaz; he's the most junior out of the lot of them, and if he's to be believed, he would have benefitted more from Darrell staying alive."

"How?"

"He was hoping to get Darrell's job when Darrell got the promotion, so it makes little sense to kill him. The most ambitious ones, from what I can see, are Carol North – possible second in line for the job – Lizzie – the leggy blonde – and Sangita – the rich kid from Mumbai. Pantoni's lower down the list, unless she's more ambitious than she lets on. The only ones I've ruled out are Gaz, and probably Matt."

"Well, you might have to put Matt back on the list because he told me he's hoping to get the promotion as well, and he openly disliked Darrell."

"The pharmaceutical industry is far more competitive than I'd imagined," said Rachel, perusing the wine bar to make sure they weren't being listened to.

"According to Matt, it is ruthless. Having told you to add him to the list, I think you should take him off again; he's an unlikely candidate."

"Make your mind up," said Rachel.

"He's too honest to be a killer, and his mum's a policewoman, his dad's a psychiatric nurse and his sister's a nurse. I can't see them bringing up a cold-blooded murderer."

Rachel chuckled. "If only it was that simple. Background plays a part in who we are, but killers don't care about such things and there's no mould."

"I suppose you're right. You're assuming the promotion is the motive. What if there's another motive, Rachel?"

"Any suggestions?" Rachel asked.

"I'm not sure. What if Stoney was having an affair with Darrell, like Bernard suggested, and he was blackmailing her to get the job?"

"Good point. Except she was the only one not at the nightclub."

"That we know of."

"Although, if that were the case, Earl Spence could have taken matters into his own hands. He's very protective of Dr Stone in general, and the company in particular, but I'm sure his motivation is money and stock market shares rather than genuine concern. It will be interesting to investigate how the shares are divvied up. He didn't like Darrell, but I'm sure he could have blocked his promotion without resorting to murder."

Rachel turned her head as a crowd entered the wine bar. "I think it might be time to find somewhere quieter."

"Good idea," said Sarah, standing.

"I didn't mean you couldn't finish your cocktail."

Sarah supped the rest of her drink and placed the glass on the table. "I'm ready. To be honest, I'm glad not to be drinking the stuff Matt left. Give me a cheap bottle of German wine any day."

"Or a Pernod." Rachel squeezed Sarah's arm.

"Definitely one of those. Let's eat in the Steak House, shall we?"

Rachel wasn't as keen on red meat as her friend but was always happy to eat a steak at least once on every cruise.

"You're on," she said, taking her arm.

They walked through the busy atrium, negotiating their way through crowds of passengers either heading to dinner or going for an evening out. A brass band played in the lower part of the atrium with passengers crowding the stairs to listen in. A few were dancing on the small dance floor below, while others casually chatted.

They climbed up one flight of stairs to the third tier of the atrium before turning left towards the Steak House.

Here, the crowds thinned out and the music became more of a distant hum.

"This is what I love about cruising: there's something for everyone," said Rachel. "Are you enjoying being back?" The question was innocent enough, but she felt Sarah stiffen. "Is everything okay?"

Sarah sighed. "I think so. It's just been hard getting back into the routine as a married woman. I'm still Nurse Bradshaw at work, and the team is great. In that sense, nothing's changed."

"I feel a 'however' coming on," prompted Rachel.

"I didn't want to say anything with all that's going on with you and Carlos, and now the investigation."

"What is it, Sarah?"

Sarah bit her bottom lip. "You might as well know, I suppose. Being Mrs Bradshaw-Goodridge isn't going quite as well as I'd hoped."

They strolled into the restaurant and asked for a quiet table in the corner. The waiter obliged, ensuring they had privacy. He would assume it was because Sarah was in uniform and didn't want to attract attention.

Once they were seated and the waiter had taken the order for drinks, Rachel scrutinised Sarah's face.

"Tell me what's troubling you."

Sarah stared vacantly at the menu for a moment or two before looking up. "You know how I always said Jason would make the perfect husband once he got over his previous rejection?"

"Yes." Rachel nodded. "At the wedding, you said you were the luckiest woman alive."

"Well, I still am, but…"

"But what?"

"He's changed."

"How?"

"You saw how he behaved last night, Rachel. He's not the same man; he's stressy, jealous of everyone and possessive. I thought after we married he'd be more secure, not less."

"And you're sure you're not making this out to be a bigger problem than it is?"

"Quite sure." Sarah shook her head. "He's been moody, snappish and downright nasty."

"To you?"

"Moody, yes, but not nasty to me. He's had a go at others, though. He hangs around the medical centre when he's off duty, checking who I'm seeing. Bernard laughs it off and tells me he's a man in love, but he's brooding. Even his relationship with Waverley isn't as good as it was."

"Has Waverley mentioned it?"

"He wouldn't do that. I've just seen the way he looks at Jason sometimes, particularly when Jason snaps. It's sort of stupid, but I'd dreamed of becoming a wife so often when we were together. I imagined we'd carry on the way we always had, except closer."

"It's not always easy once the initial excitement wears off," agreed Rachel. "But you become closer as time goes on. At least, you do if your husband doesn't go off to China pretending to be married to a beautiful woman." Rachel forced a smile at the irony.

"I know I shouldn't worry about it. He had such a bad upbringing with his parents; they didn't set him a great example, and then with his fiancée going off with his best friend… I'm sure he'll adapt. Perhaps he just needs more time."

The waiter returned with a martini and lemonade for Rachel and a soda and lime for Sarah. They ordered T-bone steaks, Sarah's medium and Rachel's well done. Rachel asked for salad and sweet potato, and Sarah requested salad and fries.

Once the waiter left, Rachel said, "You've only been married a few months, Sarah. Give it time. He'll be the Jason you married soon enough."

Sarah bit her lip again. "I hope so."

Rachel reached out, taking Sarah's hand in hers. "Look at me, Sarah."

Sarah stopped the lip biting and reluctantly lifted her reddening eyelids.

"Jason loves you more than anything else, and you love him. Yes, he's been burned in the past, and yes, he might struggle with balancing his job with married life, but he's grounded in every other way. He'll get there. I know he will."

"What about the jealousy? It's suffocating. He's even been off with Bernard when he won't tell him about every man I've seen. I don't know whether he thinks we're spending too much time together."

Rachel thought for a moment. She had never taken Jason for the overbearing sort and wondered whether there was more to it.

"When did it start?"

"A few weeks after we started the new contract as a married couple."

"And did anything trigger it?"

Their dinners arrived at the table, and Sarah sat back, concentrating.

"Can I get you any sauces, ladies?" the waiter asked.

"French mustard for me," said Rachel.

"I'll have English mustard and tomato ketchup, please," said Sarah.

Once the accompaniments arrived, Sarah spoke. "I can't think of anything that sparked it off, but Jason isn't always forthcoming. He keeps things to himself. You know me, Rachel. I'm not a flirt, but I'm friendly; as you are. These days, I worry every time I speak to someone of the opposite sex; sometimes even with women."

Rachel pondered. "Have you told Jason how his behaviour is making you feel?"

"I tried to last night when we got back to the ship, but his damned bleep went off. I think that might be part of the problem. Every time we try to have a conversation, one or other of our radios interrupts us."

Rachel thought back to when she and Carlos first married and how it had been difficult to find any degree of work-life balance. Her work as a detective was full on, and Carlos often worked away in his role as a private investigator. If she was honest, it was probably Carlos who felt the separations more keenly than she did. The only time she had ever felt any jealousy was when the goddess appeared on their honeymoon and he dropped the bombshell that he'd been a spy.

"Would you like me to have a word with him?"

"Not yet, Rachel. I think it should come from me, but if he goes into internalising mode, I may take you up on the offer. Now I think that's enough of my whinging; let's eat and talk about something else. I still want to help with the investigation if I can."

Chapter 17

Sarah's radio fired into action almost as soon as they left the restaurant. She pressed a button.

"A guest has fallen on deck sixteen. The officer on scene requests the young man is checked out. There are no obvious injuries."

"Acknowledged." Sarah sighed as she ended the short communication. "At least it won't be serious, and they had the courtesy to wait until I'd eaten," she said. "I'll see you later, Rachel."

"I hope you're not too busy tonight." Rachel yawned. "I'm heading up to my room for some shuteye. I think the jet lag's kicking in again."

"I'll see you in the morning for our visit to Goa," Sarah replied. After Rachel left, she spoke into the radio again. "I'll be a few minutes. I have to go to the medical centre first."

"I'll let the officer know."

Sarah hadn't brought the medical bag to dinner with her, an unusual lapse of concentration. She told herself off on the way down to deck two, pleased it wasn't a dire emergency. The medical centre was closed, so she used her swipe key.

Once she'd retrieved the bag, Sarah took the lift to deck sixteen. The sky was black, but there was the usual outdoor lighting, plus the benefit of a partial moon to help her on her way. A slight breeze caressed her face and she could hear the waves lapping against the side of the ship as she pressed the radio button.

"Yes, Nurse?" the operator answered.

"Sorry, what part of deck sixteen is the patient?"

"Didn't I say? I should be the one who's sorry. He's on the port bow."

"Thanks." She ended the call before muttering, "Great! The complete opposite to starboard stern." Again pleased the call wasn't urgent, Sarah dragged the medical bag – or rather, the small but heavy case – behind her.

On arrival at the front of the ship, she took a left towards the portside. It was amazing how she now navigated the enormous ship with ease without getting lost, although there were still a few mazes that challenged her. She arrived at the scene where a crewman was chatting to a young man sitting in one of the plastic deckchairs.

"Hello, Nurse," the crewman said. "The officer told me to stay here until you arrived. Is it okay if I go now? I have to finish my work."

"Yes, of course." *Poor man*, she thought, noticing he walked with a limp as he scurried away. Sarah then focused on the teenager, who didn't look injured at all. "Hello, I'm Nurse Bradshaw. Can you tell me your name, please?" She pulled out a pad to make notes.

"Carl Jacques."

"Date of birth?"

The young man replied, and Sarah took down his stateroom number in case billing was required.

"Are you allergic to anything that you know of?"

"No."

"And where are you hurt, Carl?"

"Nowhere really. It's just me pride that's hurt, Nurse Bradshaw. I told 'em not to bother you, but the officer who found me insisted you were called."

Sarah's ears pricked up. "What do you mean, found you? Were you unconscious?" She inspected his face, paying particular attention to the pupils of his eyes.

"No. I got into a bit of a fight with some bloke over a girl. I didn't tell the officer that, mind. I was just having a rest after being winded, that's all."

"This man punched you?" Sarah asked. "Where?"

Carl pulled up his shirt and pointed to the left side of his ribs. They were red, but his breathing was equal on both sides. She palpated the area and noted there was only a slight tenderness, most likely because of bruising over the red area.

"It was more of a shove and I fell into the chair, which is what took the wind out of me guts."

Sarah made some more notes before removing her stethoscope and examining his chest. "No real damage." She smiled at him. "I don't suppose you got your attacker's name?"

"He didn't introduce himself, like, but the woman told him not to be so childish. She called him Matt."

Sarah raised her eyebrows. "Can you describe him?"

"I will, but I don't want to get him into trouble, like. I was flirting with his bird."

When will men stop referring to women as birds? Sarah was beginning to empathise with his attacker. "Go on, then. Describe him."

Carl described a man who sounded exactly like Matt Wright. "I can describe the woman in a lot more detail." Carl grinned. "A gorgeous blonde with long legs."

"Thank you. I'll need to report the incident to our security team. One of them might wish to speak to you again."

"It really was nothing," Carl grimaced as he stood up, rubbing his ribs.

"All acts of violence on board are reported. It will be up to the security team to decide whether any further action is taken. Do you feel okay now you're standing?"

"Yes, Nurse."

Sarah returned the pad to its place and closed the bag.

"Is that it? Can I go now? Me dad'll be wondering where I've got to."

"Yes, you can go. Please call if you have any aftereffects. I suggest you take a non-steroidal such as ibuprofen for the bruising."

Sarah watched Carl Jacques waddling towards the nearest stairs that led down to the next deck. She waited until he was safely out of sight, and then paused to watch the reflection of the moon shining on the water from the starboard side. It was easy to get lost in reverie in moments like these. The dark black sea below, gently lit by the moonlight, created the perfect mural of the wonder of nature. Sarah inhaled the freshest air there had been since the ship left Mumbai that morning. She continued to take a few deep breaths before returning by the way she'd come, pulling the bag behind her.

Sarah's amble turned to a march when she saw a figure throwing an object over the side.

"Excuse me. You're not allowed to throw things into the ocean." Sarah arrived at the spot and peered over the side to see what had been thrown. It was then she felt a sharp pain on her right cheek. Staggering backwards, she tripped over her case and teetered, unbalanced. Pain shot through her right wrist as she put it out to break the fall and it hit the deck.

The shadowy figure was running in the opposite direction to the way she had arrived, so all she could see was their back. Sarah was lying on her side, feeling lightheaded, but she managed to turn onto her back to reach for her radio. It had landed across the deck and was out of reach. Sarah couldn't use her right hand because of the pain, but she forced herself to sit up and put her head between her legs, trying to dispel the swimming head.

She took a few deep breaths, calming herself, recovering enough to move into a position where she was sitting up with her back to the metal side of the ship. She could feel the wrist swelling and was unable to move her fingers; Sarah knew it was broken. Then burning pain over her right cheek made her wince. She reached up with her left hand and felt something wet and sticky. The blood was trickling down her white uniform.

"I say. Are you all right?"

Sarah recognised Dr Tia Stone's voice, although her face was fading in and out of focus.

"I feel a bit faint. Could you pass me the radio, please? It's over there."

Tia did as she asked her before bending down to check Sarah's face. "You're bleeding," she said.

Thanks for that, thought Sarah. She pressed the call button on the radio.

"It's Sarah Bradshaw. I've been injured, possible broken wrist. Could you send the medics, please?"

"Yes, ma'am," said the calm voice on the other end. "I'll leave the radio open until they get there."

"Is there anything in that bag that could help? I've done a little first aid." It turned out Tia was being modest and was quite the competent first aider. Before anyone arrived, she had applied a loose-fitting splint to Sarah's right wrist, cleaned her face with antiseptic, which brought tears to her eyes, and applied a pressure dressing over the wound, stemming the bleeding.

"I think you're going to need some stitches to that wound," Tia said. "What happened?"

"I'm not sure, really. Someone was throwing rubbish over the side. I called out to them because it's dangerous, and before I knew it, they must have punched me or hit me with something. I lost my balance and landed on my wrist."

"Oh dear, you're being very brave about it. I'd be a snivelling wreck. Here was I, thinking cruise holidays were safe. First dear Darrell and now this."

Sarah noticed moisture appearing in the corners of the stone-faced woman's eyes. Tia didn't seem nearly as harsh as she had on their first meeting.

"They usually are. It's the first time this has happened to me, if that's any consolation."

Tia almost smiled and seemed about to say something else, but they heard hurried footsteps approaching from the stern.

"Sarah! My goodness, what happened?" Janet Plover was the first to arrive, followed by Bernard pushing a wheelchair.

"Do you mind if I tell you when we get downstairs?"

"Of course. I'm assuming you haven't damaged your back?"

"No spinal injury. Just the wrist and the face."

"In that case, let's help you up." Bernard and Janet assisted Sarah to her feet while Tia held the wheelchair in place.

"Dr Stone's been marvellous," said Sarah. Their eyes met for a moment. "Thank you."

"Anytime, and call me Tia," she said. "Now I'll leave you in these capable hands and get back to my evening stroll. Although I might move to the deck below where there are more people around."

As soon as they were in the lift, Janet asked, "What did she mean by that last comment?" But Sarah remained tight-lipped until they were in the medical centre. Then she explained everything that had happened while Janet finely stitched her cheek.

"That shouldn't leave much of a scar," Janet said.

Gwen joined them on the ward. "I heard you were injured, Sarah," she said, concern on her face. "We'll need to call security. This needs investigating. We can't have passengers attacking an officer – or any member of the crew, for that matter."

Sarah knew better than to argue but hoped Jason wouldn't overreact.

"Thankfully it's not too deep a cut, although I think the perpetrator may have left a ring mark on your cheek. Look at the indentation," Janet said. Bernard and Gwen leaned forward, Gwen scrunching her eyes.

"You're right. Bernard, get a photo of that before it fades. I'm going to call Waverley and get him to let Jason know his wife's in treatment."

Janet waited for Bernard to take some photos before wheeling Sarah through to get an X-Ray of the wrist.

"You know it's broken, but we need to check how bad it is before putting it into a cast."

Sarah was pleased Janet kept her in the X-Ray department while the film was processed. She needed some time to consider what had happened to her before she faced a quizzing from Waverley. What worried her more than anything was how Jason would react. At least the lightheadedness had gone away, and although her face stung, it wasn't as painful as it had been. The wrist was another matter.

"You'll be pleased to hear it's a straightforward radial fracture, so no need to reset it." As Janet spoke, Sarah heard voices filtering through from the ward. "Would you like me to ask Bernard to plaster it through here before you face that lot?"

Sarah bit her lip. "Yes please. Could I get a drink of water too?"

"Of course. Wait right there. I'll keep the marauders back until you're ready. Don't you worry."

True to Janet's word, Bernard appeared on his own with the plaster trolley, followed briefly by Janet with a glass of iced water.

"Jason will be down soon. Rosemary's on her way to relieve him from brig duty. Gwen's telling Waverley what we know so far and keeping him busy. Rachel's out there with him."

"Good. Rachel will keep Jason under control when he gets here."

Janet gave her a sideways look but didn't pry. "I'll leave Bernard to patch you up."

Bernard smirked. "What colour plaster would you like, Nurse Bradshaw?"

Sarah laughed for the first time since the incident. Bernard always knew how to cheer her up.

Chapter 18

Party sounds from the main atrium reminded Rachel she was supposed to be on holiday. She paused at the top of the spiralling staircase on deck six, which gave her a good view of the activities on deck four of the atrium. A pop trio had replaced the brass band from earlier and passengers were dancing to the sounds of the eighties.

After watching the fun for a few minutes, she felt someone tapping her on the shoulder.

"Hey, Rachel. How are you?" Rosemary Inglis, the former Olympic slalom kayaker, now security officer, beamed at her.

"I'm good, thank you. What about you?"

"Busy as ever. I never imagined working on a cruise ship would be so challenging. I thought I'd spend my days keeping overenthusiastic guests in check." Rosemary laughed.

"I'm sure you get your fair share of that too," said Rachel. "I hear you've been speaking to the Rejuvenescence Pharma lot."

Rosemary grinned. "Nothing escapes your attention, does it? I'm about to brief the chief. Do you want to come along? He told me you were doing some investigating of your own, so I'm sure he won't mind. We can compare notes."

Rachel was torn between a yearning for her bed and her desire to get to the bottom of who killed Darrell Baker. She capitulated.

"Why not? I won't sleep now anyway," she said.

Waverley's eyes widened when Rachel walked in with Rosemary.

"I bumped into Rachel upstairs and thought we could pool our resources," Rosemary explained. A glimmer of disapproval passed from Waverley to his ebullient officer before he shrugged.

"May as well. Do either of you want a drink? I'm having a small Scotch before turning in for the night." Rachel interpreted that as 'be brief, I haven't got all night.' It also implied there wasn't much to share.

"I'll have still water, please, if you've got any."

"Now that I have." He turned to a water dispenser in the corner of his office and poured her a glass before removing ice from his small fridge and adding it to the water. "What about you, Inglis?"

"I'm fine, sir. I've not long had a coffee."

Rachel assumed Rosemary was on call for the security team. She took the glass from Waverley, who indicated they should sit around his communal table rather than his desk. He got straight to the point.

"What have you got, Inglis?"

"Not a lot. No-one I spoke to admits to seeing Mr Baker after he left the nightclub."

Waverley frowned. "Same response I got, then. What about Gary Jacobs? It seems he was the last person to see the man alive."

"He doesn't remember what happened. In fact, he doesn't even remember going outside the club with Mr Baker on the night in question. His story is fuzzy. He thought the argument happened inside, but he remembers being told to get lost. The trouble is, with some of the others telling him what they saw, his recollections have become muddled with theirs. It's hard to distinguish what really happened from what has been suggested."

Waverley huffed. "From what I can gather, the rest of them also had a few drinks, but they all say Baker left with Jacobs, so we have to assume that's when the argument occurred. Ten to twenty minutes later, Jacobs reappears and resumes his drinking. Is that the impression you've got?"

"Yes, sir." Rosemary appeared hesitant.

"Say what's on your mind," Waverley instructed.

"I think they all seem too clear on that one point. It's almost as if that part of their stories is rehearsed, whereas the rest of the evening's events are more hazy."

"Good God! Don't tell me you think they're all in on it?"

"No, sir, I don't. I just think it's odd, that's all. Maybe they're taking the path of least resistance to protect their own skins."

Waverley nodded. "Ah, I see what you're getting at. That would make more sense. What did the people you interviewed tell you was the reason for going outside separately?"

This was news to Rachel, and her ears pricked up. "After Darrell left?" she quizzed.

"Yes, and after Jacobs returned," Waverley clarified.

"I think I've got to the bottom of that. Most of them reckon they went out for a breath of fresh air. The only one who cracked was Carol North. She says one of them – Matthew Wright – had got hold of some ganga – cannabis to us – and they took turns to go outside to smoke a joint."

"All of them?" Rachel quizzed.

"According to Carol, all except Dr Pantoni and Earl Spence. What did they say they were doing?" Rosemary checked with Waverley.

"Getting a breath of fresh air. They're taking us for damn fools and lying through their teeth. I haven't got the patience for this. We will interview them all again tomorrow. I'm not having any more of this nonsense." Waverley's face had turned purple. He threw back the rest of his whisky while looking at Rachel expectantly.

"While I think of it," she said, "when you interview them again, could you find out if it's usual to give out prepaid credit cards, and if not, why Carol gave one to Gaz? That's the reason he got so drunk. Other than that, I'm sorry. I didn't find out very much at all, other than what we know already.

"Gaz – that's Gary Jacobs – believes Darrell was drugged when they were at the O Pedro as I suggested. From what the others say, Darrell was highly ambitious and was in line for the promotion until the start of the holiday. I believe Earl Spence may have persuaded Dr Stone to make this team-building holiday a selection process. In a way, that's why we've ended up with a dead body. Unless…"

"Unless what?" Waverley snapped.

"It could be the perpetrator planned to kill Darrell prior to the moving of the goalposts. To get rid of the competition."

"So why go ahead with the plan once the field opened up?" Waverley looked thoughtful.

"I don't know. Perhaps the person in question thought he would still get the job. If that theory is correct, Earl Spence and Dr Stone – who was an unlikely suspect anyway – are in the clear. If only we knew more."

"Indeed," said Waverley. "We have to assume they are all suspects for now apart from Dr Stone, who has a cast-iron alibi. She was chairing a conference call around the world at the time Baker left the nightclub, and she didn't leave the ship. We have her boarding at midnight and not going ashore again."

"What time did the others get back?" Rachel asked.

"Ah, now here is an interesting part. Most of them returned at three-thirty in the morning. They swiped in within minutes of each other, including Jacobs. His colleagues must have helped him on board. However, Mr Spence and Miss Regum boarded within fifteen minutes of each other, she at 05:25 and he at 05:40."

"Implying they were together but pretending not to be," Rosemary finished.

"No wonder he was out jogging so early," said Rachel. "He hadn't been to bed."

Waverley cleared his throat, embarrassed. Rosemary chuckled.

"Not to sleep anyway."

"What reason did they give for returning later than the others?" Rachel asked.

"Er, I haven't asked. If they are having a liaison, that's their business and has no bearing on the investigation. We can't go around exposing every illicit affair that goes on or we'd never stop."

"He's sixty, and she's twenty-five with a powerful father. Mr Regum could cause one hell of a stink if he found out," said Rosemary.

"Thank you, Inglis. I think that's all for now." Waverley stood. The meeting was over and Rachel realised they had probably told her more than Waverley wanted her to know.

Rachel placed her half-full glass down on the table, frowning. Would Sangita really be so ambitious that she'd spend a few hours on a cheap date with a man older than her own father? People did some crazy things to get to the top. She hadn't warmed to the younger woman, but she hadn't thought her stupid.

I wonder if she has blackmail in mind, she thought.

Rosemary had just reached the door when Waverley's telephone rang.

"Hang on, Inglis, just in case," he said, lifting the receiver. "*What*? When?"

Rachel stopped dead when she saw the colour drain from his face.

"Right. I'll be right down."

"Am I needed, sir?" Rosemary asked.

"Yes… No… I mean, yes." He was stuttering. "Sarah's been attacked."

He held his hand up to stop Rachel from interrupting. Her heart raced; her jaw dropped. She could barely breathe as a horrible thought crossed her mind.

"She's injured but not badly. She's had some stitches to her face and sustained a broken wrist."

Rachel found she'd been holding her breath as relief swept through her body. How had she even thought the unimaginable?

"Who would attack Sarah?"

"That's what we're going to find out. Inglis, can you go and tell Goodridge face-to-face, and relieve him from brig duty?

"On second thoughts, wait. He'll take it badly. First, go up to deck sixteen portside bow, which is where the attack happened. There'll be some blood. Seal off the area – make out it's being cleaned or something; don't draw attention to the crime. We'll examine it in the morning. After that, go and tell Goodridge. Make sure he doesn't attack Maku."

"Why would Jason attack someone?" Rachel's mind was reeling as she followed Waverley towards the medical centre.

Waverley sighed heavily. "Goodridge hasn't been himself lately, verging on insubordinate at times. I've let it go, giving him time to talk to me when he's ready. I'm pleased to say he did just that earlier this evening. Well, pleased isn't the right word, but I'm glad he got around to it."

"And this has something to do with the person in the brig?"

"Yes. Goodridge's uncovered a gambling syndicate and he believes this Maku is the ringleader. They target passengers who have a weakness for the gambling table and invite them to a private room where they can bet higher amounts in cash. There's a lot of money involved and they have fleeced vulnerable passengers."

"I still don't understand why Jason would attack the man you've arrested."

Waverley was still moving fast with Rachel keeping pace. "He's been getting secret messages threatening to harm Sarah if he doesn't leave it be."

Rachel's heart thumped inside her chest. "And this man, Maku, could be responsible for tonight's attack?"

"It's hard to say. We're deporting him tomorrow for beating his girlfriend. I agreed with Goodridge that we'll stick to that charge for now. We don't have enough evidence that he's the head of this syndicate anyway, and once I knew Sarah was under threat, I didn't want to take any chances. I thought lessening the punishment would be enough to cut off the head and close the syndicate."

"Thank goodness Rosemary's as strong as a battalion," said Rachel.

"You understand now why I sent her personally rather than calling him?" Waverley's voice was grim. "But if Maku has had anything to do with Sarah's injuries, I swear I'll let Goodridge in the room with him and walk away."

Rachel knew Waverley would never do such a thing, so let the comment made in the heat of the moment go. After all, she wasn't feeling any less angry herself.

They arrived at the medical centre and Waverley burst through the door. Gwen Sumner was waiting for him. Waverley marched past her into the infirmary.

"Where is she?"

Gwen tried to calm the security chief, who was firing a barrage of questions. A few moments later, Janet Plover appeared through the far side door.

"Sarah's having a plaster cast applied to her wrist and needs a little time to get treatment." Rachel took that to mean her friend needed some time to recover before facing Waverley, and most probably Jason.

"Come into my office and Janet and I will fill you in on what she's told us so far," Gwen said.

Janet was helping corral Waverley into Gwen's office when he barged past them. Gwen followed him inside, giving Rachel an opportunity to speak to Janet.

"How is she? What would you like me to do?" she asked the doctor.

"She's okay. A bit shocked, but she'll be fine. Could you stick around? Sarah wants you here when Jason arrives, so why don't you join us in Gwen's office and hear what she's told us? It'll save her having to repeat the story several times." Janet put an arm around Rachel's shoulder and fixed her gaze, compassion oozing from her. "Trust me. She's going to be okay."

Rachel took a few deep breaths and allowed herself to be drawn into Gwen's office. Her biggest fear – that this was somehow her fault – caused her throat to tighten. Why hadn't she challenged Jason after Sarah told her about his behaviour? She would have been glued to her friend's side if she'd had any inkling Sarah was in danger. No wonder Jason has been so suffocating and protective. She should have known it was more than petty jealousy.

As soon as she entered the senior nurse's office, Gwen handed her a brandy.

Chapter 19

Gwen related the story Sarah had given the medical team after they had admitted her to the infirmary. Relief flowed through Rachel's tense limbs on hearing Sarah had been the victim of a random rather than a targeted attack. There was no way the person who hit Sarah could have planned it, or known where she would be. Neither could they have expected she would challenge them for throwing litter over the side.

Waverley also seemed relieved, but he still sounded concerned. "I don't like the thought of someone being so brazen as to attack one of our nurses over an episode of litter louting."

"We can all agree on that," said Gwen.

They heard the medical centre's bell ring, interrupting the conversation. "That will be Jason," said Janet. "Would you two like to brief him before anyone sees Sarah? I'm sure she'll be back on the ward now."

Waverley was still frantically writing notes and appeared hesitant. He looked up at Rachel.

"I'll talk to him," said Rachel, getting up.

As soon as she opened the door, she realised Jason would not be reassured easily. He stopped on seeing her, wide-eyed and breathless.

"How is she? Where is she?"

Rachel blocked the entrance. "I haven't seen her yet, but Janet assures me she's fine and they'll be moving her to the ward any minute now." Putting the palms of her hands on his chest to get his full attention, she looked into his frantic eyes and spoke steadily. "It wasn't a targeted attack, Jason. It's not your fault."

His shoulders sagged; the tension in his jaw eased as he swallowed hard. Moisture filled his wild eyes.

"Are you sure?"

"Positive. And to be honest, I was playing the same self-blame game. However, there's no-one to blame other than the person who hit her. Come and sit down for a few minutes, and I'll walk you through what she told the medics."

Jason followed her into the room where passengers and crew normally waited to be seen by a nurse or a doctor. She explained how, after they had eaten dinner, Sarah was called to see a passenger who'd fallen.

"After she dealt with the patient, Sarah saw someone throwing what she assumed was litter over the side and approached them to tell them they weren't allowed to do that. When she got near, the passenger – she believes it was a passenger – hit out and struck her in the face. Sarah stumbled backwards and tripped over the medical bag, landing badly on her right wrist. It's broken, and she's got a cut to her cheek which has been repaired, but other than that, Janet assures me she's fine."

Jason put his head in his hands, shoulders heaving as he sobbed. "I thought it was—"

"I know. Waverley told me about the threats. You should have said something, Jason."

"And freak her out?" He continued crying into his hands, shaking his head.

"Your behaviour's been freaking her out anyway. You're married now. You have to communicate even when things are bad."

"I was trying to protect her."

Crouching down in front of him, Rachel pulled him into a hug. "I know you were." Enough had been said for now. She lifted his head up. "Come on. Let's go and see your wife."

Jason wiped his face on his sleeve and blinked away any remaining tears.

"I'd like that," he said.

Rachel had noticed Waverley and Gwen hovering in the background while she dealt with the distraught man. Jason caught sight of his boss.

"Sorry, sir."

"You've got nothing to be sorry about, man. You go ahead and we'll follow in a few minutes. I'll give Inglis a bell while you're gone."

"You come too, Rachel. She'll want to see you," Jason said.

Sarah was sitting up in bed, bantering with Bernard when they walked in.

"I'll get you that brandy now the cavalry is here," Bernard joked.

Jason strode across the room, sat on the bed, and kissed Sarah gently on the lips. "I'm so sorry for my behaviour. I'll explain everything once you're out of here."

Sarah gave Rachel a confused but relieved glance before rubbing his cheek with the palm of her left hand.

"Whatever it is, I'm sure you had your reasons."

Waverley and Bernard joined them a few minutes later. Bernard handed Sarah a glass of brandy.

"Are you sure you don't want a Stinger? You'd feel no pain afterwards."

"Apart from the burning in my gullet, you mean? No, thank you."

They all burst out laughing. Bernard was a great person to have around when tension was in the air.

Rachel watched her friend closely while she repeated the story Gwen had already told them. There was nothing new to add, apart from an extra bit they hadn't been told: Tia Stone had come to her rescue and administered first aid.

"She's actually quite nice beneath the bristly exterior. Very calm in a crisis," Sarah explained. "I owe her. Who knows how long I'd have been sitting there if she hadn't come along. My radio had fallen out of reach and I was too dizzy to get to it."

Bernard chuckled. "I don't expect you get to be CEO of an expanding pharmaceutical company if you can't apply a splint and a band-aid."

Rachel couldn't help wondering whether it was sheer coincidence that someone from the pharmaceutical lot seemed to appear whenever there was trouble, but she said nothing. She was more determined than ever to find out what had happened to Darrell, even though it appeared Sarah's attack had nothing to do with the investigation. She would also be pleased when the head of the gambling syndicate was removed from the ship the next day, certain it would be enough of a warning to his fellow criminals to end that racket.

"You're quiet, Rachel. What's up?" Sarah asked.

"Nothing. I'm just happy you're okay. I'll cancel our tour in the morning."

"You'll do no such thing. I assume I'm fit for discharge, Janet?"

Janet Plover had come in with Gwen and heard the end of the conversation.

"There's no reason to keep you in the infirmary. I'm sure Jason will get the rest of the night off to take care of you, and you can go ashore tomorrow if you feel well enough. It might do you good."

"That's settled, then." Sarah had a determined look in her eyes. Even Jason decided not to argue.

"You take the rest of the week off, Sarah. You're due some leave anyway. I'm sure Bernard and Brigitte will cover, and I can take some extra on-calls," said Gwen. "Then you can return to light duties until your wrist heals. You do my job and I'll do yours."

"That I've got to see," said Bernard, laughing.

"Watch it, Nurse Guinto, or you'll be working double-time," Gwen warned.

Bernard saluted. "I'll take the rest of your on-call tonight, Sarah. I'll let reception know so you can turn your radio off."

"I don't suppose you have anything on my attacker?" Sarah checked with Waverley.

"Not yet. We'll see what CCTV footage we can find and examine the scene in the morning. Inglis has sealed off the area where the attack took place. We'll examine it as soon as it's light and get it cleaned up. I don't expect to find anything, but you never know. Your assailant might have dropped something. Inglis had a quick scout around with a torch but couldn't find anything."

Rachel was delighted to see the colour returning to Sarah's face. She had looked deathly pale when they walked in. In fact, the atmosphere had changed from acute anxiety to almost cheerful, the lightening of the mood mostly down to Bernard's quick wit.

"I almost forgot to mention," he said. "You can't see it now, but Janet noticed an indentation on Sarah's right cheek. Gwen told me to take some photos." He led Waverley and Rachel over to the computer at the side of the infirmary and showed them some images on the screen. "We think it's a mark from a ring."

"A woman's ring, by the looks of it," said Waverley.

Rachel's heart sank. She was certain she had seen something like that over the past couple of days but couldn't place it. Had she got Sarah involved in someone's sinister game after all?

"It's not much to go on, but at least we have something," said Waverley. "Good job, you two." He patted Bernard on the head and gave Gwen a respectful nod. "Now, if you don't mind, I promised my wife I'd join her for a nightcap two hours ago."

"Oh dear. You'll be in the spare bed tonight," Bernard teased.

"We don't have a spare bed." Waverley looked concerned. "We have a bed settee, though, so I'd best be off. See you in the morning, Goodridge. Inglis will make sure our charge stays where he is. I'll get Ravanos to cover her on-call. You take care of our patient."

"Thank you, sir."

"I'm sorry this happened to you, Sarah," Waverley added. "We'll do everything we can to find who's responsible."

After Waverley left, Sarah polished off the brandy and sat gingerly on the edge of the bed. Jason sat next to her and assisted her to her feet. Rachel and the others watched as he supported her gently with a muscular arm around her waist. Her right arm was in a sling and she leaned on him, more for comfort than support, Rachel suspected.

Gwen's eyes followed them. "That was a nasty business. I hope Waverley finds who did it and throws them off. At least it wasn't any more serious, and Sarah came out of it better than she might have if the passenger had been more malicious. It's so rare for a nurse to be attacked unless dealing with people under the influence, but then security is around to restrain them. I'm just pleased she's not in any more danger." Gwen went on, "If you guys don't mind, I'll call it a night."

"No problem, boss. Me and Janet will manage. Where's the big boss tonight?"

"If you're referring to Graham, after dinner he went for a drink with Captain Jenson. I'll update him in the morning."

Bernard opened his mouth, Rachel guessed to make some joke about Gwen and Dr Bentley, but snapped it shut just in time.

"I'm going to call it a night too," said Rachel. "Goodnight." She exited with Gwen and headed upstairs with a horrible feeling that things had just got a whole lot worse.

Chapter 20

It was 5am when Rachel woke with fear clutching at her chest; the bed was soaked in sweat. She shot upright, breathless and panicky. In her dream, Carlos was in danger and calling for her. Helena was lying dead next to him, eyes wide open.

Realising it was just a dream, Rachel flopped her head back down on the pillow. If only there was a way to contact Carlos without putting him in danger. Instead, she had to do what she'd done every day since he went away. She would write to him and store the letter in a folder for him to read if... no... *when* he came home. Right now, though, a strong coffee was required.

Forty minutes after her shock awakening, Rachel was on deck sixteen. It was still dark. The ship had docked half an hour earlier and dim lights from the dock helped in her quest. The running track was well lit, but that's not where she was heading this morning.

Rachel arrived at the cordoned off 'for cleaning' area, having a quick look around, not expecting to find anything. Rosemary Inglis was thorough, and if there had been something to find the security officer would have found it. Rachel quivered on eyeing the dark patch left by Sarah's blood, anger rising inside. Then she peered over the side rail. This part of deck sixteen was above the wider deck fifteen. Whatever Sarah's attacker had thrown over the side might be somewhere on the deck below where she was standing. First, though, she wanted to check the gulleys on this deck and follow in the footsteps Sarah said her assailant had run. As expected, there was nothing to be found.

Rachel took the outside steps down to deck fifteen and began another search directly below where the attack had taken place. This search, too, turned out to be fruitless. It was hard trying to find anything in the dark, especially when she didn't know what she was looking for. Frustrated, Rachel headed to the buffet for an early breakfast.

It was busy, she assumed because a lot of people were booked on early trips. She and Sarah weren't due to leave until ten, which gave her a few hours to kill. Sarah had put on a brave face following her attack, but Rachel knew it would have shaken her to the core. Her friend was anti-violence and wouldn't harm a mosquito. It wasn't fair that innocents like Sarah became victims of callous individuals who thought nothing of the damage they caused.

Rachel spent most of her time in her day job interviewing relatives of murder victims. Merciless killers who thought it was okay to take a life destroyed the families' lives as well. It wasn't okay, and Rachel would not stop until she unearthed Darrell's killer, Sarah's attacker and any criminal she had to hunt in the day job. That's what kept her going.

She hoped Sarah had slept okay and wasn't in too much pain. The incident had reminded her of the time on her first cruise when she herself had broken an ankle, saving the life of her dear friend Lady Marjorie Snellthorpe. *One of these days*, her inner voice told her, *you're going to put yourself in harm's way once too often*. Rachel stood motionless in front of the fresh fruit bar with too many puzzles going around her brain.

"Good morning, Rachel."

Rachel jumped. "Gaz! You really shouldn't sneak up on people like that."

He grinned. "And you shouldn't hold up the queue." Rachel looked behind her, and realised she was preventing several people from progressing; they were all waiting for her to make her selection.

"Whoops. Sorry." She hurriedly filled a bowl with grapefruit, adding melon and papaya for good measure.

"I tried to find you last night after I got out of a dreary meeting but couldn't. Did you have an early night?"

"No. I had dinner with my friend."

"The female nurse, I'll allow, but not the male." He grinned again.

"I was with Sarah. What time was your meeting?"

"Six to eight. Why?"

"No reason. Are you joining me for breakfast? There's a table by the window."

"I'd love to." His eyes looked hopeful, and she felt almost sorry for him. "I'll grab a fry up and be right over."

Rachel waited for Gaz to finish shovelling food into his mouth as though he hadn't eaten in weeks before she could start a proper conversation. He waxed lyrical about the food on board the ship. Recalling her first cruise and how the opulence of the ship and wonderful cuisine had left its mark, she realised it was unfair not to allow him the same privilege. Food on board the *Coral Queen* was as good as that served in any Michelin starred restaurant as far as she was concerned. Not that she'd been to a Michelin starred restaurant, so perhaps she had better park that opinion until she had.

Finally, Gaz wiped his mouth on a napkin.

"That was delicious."

"So you said," Rachel replied.

"Sorry. I'm really not used to this type of food. It's bangers and mash at me parents' house with the odd Irish stew thrown in."

"I didn't realise you still lived at home."

"I can't leave me mam until I get married. She'd never get over it. If she cramps me love life too much, I'll rent a place and not tell her about it. Not that there's much danger of that. My girlfriend is traditional like; sometimes, I think we're more friends than lovers. We've grown up together. After this cruise, I'm hoping to get away a lot more, and now Darrell's job has come up in New York, I'll apply."

What a ruthless thing to say, thought Rachel. Darrell had only been dead a matter of days and already he'd been forgotten.

"And break your mother's heart," she said.

"Nah. She won't mind me leaving if it's for a promotion. Besides, she's always saying how she'd like to visit America. Maybe I could take on Darrell's apartment."

Rachel gave him a hard stare. "You've got it all worked out, haven't you?"

Gaz lowered his eyes. "I don't mean I'm glad he's dead or anything like that. If he'd got the promotion, I'd have gone for his job anyway. I told you, me parents are ambitious for me. If I went to New York and got a senior role, I'd be able to do some cordon bleu training on the side. Maybe one day I'll be a famous chef. I've managed to get an hour with one of the chefs on board the ship. He's going to give me a few tips."

Rachel couldn't stay angry with Gaz for long. His guileless eyes sparkled whenever he spoke of cooking. It was obvious that was his real passion, so why not seize the opportunity if he could? It's not as though he and Darrell were close. They only met properly a few days ago.

"Good for you. I hope, if you do get a top chef's position, I'll be able to sample the food one day."

His ready grin was back. "I'd love you to."

"What would your girlfriend do if you moved to New York?"

"Nothing. I'd be doing us both a favour. We could get on with our lives without the family expectations."

"I see," said Rachel, thinking Gaz's relationship was sounding like an arranged marriage. "Why were you looking for me last night? Didn't you go out with your friends after your meeting?"

"They're not me friends. I don't fit in. They're too busy vying for the promotion. Earl made it clear last night that it would go to one of them and it was down to them to prove themselves worthy."

"Was Dr Stone in the meeting?"

"Aye, Stoney was there all right, but not there, if you know what I mean? She was quiet like. Silent as a—"

"Mouse?" Rachel offered.

"As a stone." Gaz laughed loudly.

"Good one. Why do you think she was quiet?"

"Dunno. Maybe this death thing hit her harder than the rest of us. She liked Darrell. Not *like*, like, you know, just liked."

"I understand. So, did any of the others go out together after the meeting?"

"Who knows? I expect some of 'em did; either that, or they were plotting. Sangie's up to something with Earl. She's far too young for him. He'll only use her."

"What makes you think they're up to something?" Rachel asked.

"Lots of secret eye contact. Matt noticed it first, and ever since he told me, I've picked up on it too. Matt's dad's a psychiatric something or other, and his mum's a cop. He's got an eye for these things."

"Are you sure Matt's not jealous? Perhaps he fancies Sangita himself."

"Nah. If there's anyone he's hoping to get off with, it's Carol. At least he was until the promotion became more of an open field. I guess he'll do his best to snuff out the competition now."

"Not a good choice of words under the circumstances," said Rachel.

"I guess not, but I can't see any of us getting mugged on board a ship."

"Is that what you think happened to Darrell?" Rachel watched for a reaction and was pleased to get one.

Gaz became much more serious. "It must have. I told you, I thought someone drugged him in the restaurant. Maybe they followed us to the nightclub and tried to rob him after we left."

Rachel decided to play her hand. "Weren't you the last one to see him alive?"

Gaz's face paled. Even beneath the sunburn, she could see he was shaken.

"You can't think I had anything to do with his death, Rachel? I've sussed why you're asking all these questions. Sangie told me to watch out for you – that you were always hanging around, watching us."

"Did she now? That's very interesting."

"For all I know, you were the one to do him in."

Rachel chuckled. "That's an odd thing to suggest. If it puts your mind at ease, I was on board the ship by midnight along with three friends, one of whom is a security officer."

"Oh, I get it now. He's got you snooping around for him, seeing what you can find out." Gaz relaxed. "I'd be glad to help if I can because I don't want anyone thinking I killed my mate."

He's your mate now, Rachel thought, but said, "You could start by telling me everything you remember about the night Darrell died. Some memories must have come back to you by now."

Gaz leaned back in his chair. "It's still hazy, but I do remember a few snippets. Like flashbacks, they keep coming back."

"Go on," said Rachel.

"I definitely think someone drugged Darrell, and if it wasn't some random guy from the restaurant, then it had to be one of us. It wasn't Stoney, 'cos she didn't arrive until after he started acting up."

Rachel had already excluded Dr Stone as a suspect, although she would like to know why she put so much pressure on the group if it was Darrell she wanted for the promotion in the first place.

"I can't prove it, but I think it might have been Carol that did it."

"What makes you say that?"

"Part of the argument me and Darrell had – it *was* outside the nightclub; came back to me this morning. He told me to shove off because I was feeding information back to Lizzie. He called me a treacherous spy.

"I tried to talk sense into him, but he said Carol told him exactly what I was up to and he wanted nothing else to do with me. Then he shoved me away. I tried to grab his arm and tell him Carol was lying, but he shoved me again. Harder that time. Then I got angry and said he could believe what he liked, that I didn't care. After the argument, I went back to the bar to drown me sorrows. Sorry if I said different before, but I swear, Rachel: that was the last time I saw him."

"Did Darrell say where he was going?"

"No, and I don't remember much else. I only know from what Lizzie said that they brought me back to the ship in a taxi. Apparently, Matt walked – or rather, carried me to my room."

"Did you all come back together?"

Gaz smirked. "No. That's another thing. Matt told me Sangie said she'd left her bag in the club, so Earl told us to go on and he'd make sure she got back safely. That might have been when they started collaborating or snogging, you know.

"Back to Carol, though. I asked the others on the quiet whether any of them were given prepaid credit cards on the night, and Matt said no. They had to put expenses through in the normal way."

That's another question answered, thought Rachel. "Perhaps Carol was being generous; presumably you don't earn as much as the rest of the team."

A look of disbelief crossed Gaz's face. "You've gotta be kidding. She's as tight as they come. Nope, I think she knew I'd get wasted, so it had to be her that drugged Darrell. Then she turned him against me and waited for her opportunity. If anyone from our lot killed him – and I still think it's farfetched; I'm sure it was some mugging gone wrong – then it was her, Carol North."

"What about me?" Carol appeared behind Gaz, who was visibly shaken by her sudden arrival.

"He was just telling me how he thought you would be the ideal person to get a promotion your company is offering."

Carol appeared pleased and slapped him on the back. "He's so right," she said.

"How are the knees?" Rachel asked.

"What do you mean? Oh yes. You're the one who turns up whenever there's a mishap. First in the caves, then at the square, and then the night Darrell died. I'd steer clear if I were you, Gaz. She's a bad omen."

Carol headed to another table not too far away while Gaz stared after her.

"Did she hear what I said?"

"No," said Rachel. "But watch your back. I'd better be going." As she left the buffet with plenty to think about, she smirked.

I sincerely hope I'm your 'bad omen', Carol North. You're on my hit list.

Chapter 21

The Goan beach was picture-postcard beautiful. When Sarah suggested they cancel their organised tour and head to the beach instead, Rachel had been slightly disappointed not to visit the historical places of interest they had previously planned to see. Now they were lounging on sun beds in gorgeous sunshine with waves lapping against the shore, she found herself content.

The beach was busy, but not horrendously so, and plenty of swaying palms at the top end provided shelter from the sun if they needed it. Sarah wore a large surgical glove over her right hand and forearm to prevent sand riding up under the plaster, which would become an unbearable irritation. The two of them lay in companionable silence, looking out to sea, watching people swimming and children playing.

"This is the first time I've seen you relaxed this cruise," said Sarah.

"It's gorgeous here. I'm glad you suggested we rest up for the day. How's the wrist?"

"Not as sore as the face, actually." Sarah tilted her hat to protect her right cheek from the sun.

"It's usually me getting on the wrong side of criminals, not you," Rachel said bashfully.

"I don't know how you do it: putting yourself in harm's way all the time. How do you keep your spirits up when there's always another bad person waiting to take over from the ones you catch?"

"Jason told you about the crime syndicate and why he's been overprotective, then?" said Rachel.

Sarah nodded, a glumness overshadowing her usually sunny disposition. "I sometimes wonder if my mum's right. Perhaps it's time to give up being a ship's nurse and settle down nearer home."

Rachel laughed. "You'd hate it!"

"You're right, but at least Jason would be safe. I worry about him like I worry about you. What if one of these times it's him who's attacked, maybe by a gang?"

"Come on, Sarah. Don't be so morose. Yes, there are criminals on board the *Coral Queen* sometimes, but it's no worse than a small town of this size. At least you can chuck the offenders off at the next port. Think of all the people whose lives are terrorised by yobs – like the ones the police have to deal with. Yes, they can be served with Civil Injunctions and CBOs, but we can't kick them out like you can."

Sarah smiled. "CBOs? Is that Criminal Behaviour Orders?"

"Yep," said Rachel.

"When you put it like that, cruise ships have the advantage. Although we're just shifting the problem somewhere else unless the authorities are involved."

Rachel grinned. "I know it doesn't sound right, but sometimes, I think I could live with that."

"You don't fool me, Rachel. I know you believe in the rehabilitation of offenders."

Rachel stared out to sea and wondered if she did still believed it was possible for people to change. She had seen some horrible things over the past few years. Things that kept her awake at night.

"I sometimes wonder if taking Waverley and Captain Jenson up on a job offer might be a good move."

Sarah's mouth opened. "You'd hate being cooped up on a ship all the time. I like it. When I'm not being threatened or attacked, that is, and don't get me wrong, I'd love you and Carlos to join us. I just can't see either of you settling into a life at sea. You're free spirits, and while I understand you're anxious about him right now, he's still the man you married. And, if I dare say, on balance, you're the one who throws yourself in front of fast-moving cars."

"You could have a point there." They both threw their heads back, laughing. "On the subject of moving cars and Darrell Baker, I had an interesting conversation with Gaz over breakfast. He still thinks it was a mugging but also says if one of them was involved, then Carol North's the culprit."

Rachel mentioned nothing about this now, but she wondered if it might have been Carol who'd attacked Sarah the night before. She didn't have the proof or motive for that, but if Carol was involved, that woman had better watch out. Rachel could be an avenging angel when she wanted to be.

"You suddenly look serious. Do you think he's right?"

"It's hard to say at the minute, but she is the one who gave Gaz the prepaid credit card, and when he checked with the others he found out it isn't the norm. Why did she want him to get plastered? Also, Carol's the person everyone believes was second in line behind Darrell for the stupid promotion, which gives her the strongest motive. If I get the chance, I'll ask Waverley to look into her background, that's for sure. But look. That's enough about murder. You need some rest. Do you fancy a paddle?"

"A bit later, perhaps. Why don't you go for a swim? I know you're itching to."

"Will you be all right? There are too many boats here to get a good swim."

Sarah gave her a look.

Rachel held her hands up. "Okay, I'll go. I'll take a stroll down to the far end of the beach, where it looks quieter."

"You do that. Before you go, would you mind just lowering this bed for me? I'm going to sunbathe for a while and finish the book I've been reading."

Rachel did as she was asked and rubbed sun cream into Sarah's exposed parts before adding a fresh dollop to herself.

"See you in a bit. I'll try not to be long."

"Take your time," said Sarah. "I'm not going anywhere."

Rachel watched as her friend turned onto her left side, put her head down on a rolled-up towel, and propped a tablet against her beach bag. Sarah looked tired and vulnerable. She hesitated, scanning the beach for nefarious people, but all she saw were holidaymakers having fun. Sarah wasn't in danger, she told herself. The bad guy, Maku, was being escorted to the airport by Indian police and in the unlikely event Carol North came across Sarah, she wouldn't attack her. Rachel was convinced last night's incident was more about what the person was throwing overboard. It was just a shame Sarah had got in the way.

Rachel ambled along the beach for twenty minutes. When she arrived at a quiet spot at the far end where there were no swimmers, she stopped. She could just see Sarah's beach bag in the distance and her friend hadn't moved. This part of the beach was close to a barrier of rocks jutting out to sea. There were no warning signs suggesting it wasn't safe to swim, but the waves were more surf like than where she and Sarah had settled. Rachel could see a few surfers further along and entered the water, leaping over the first few waves, enjoying the battle of human versus nature.

She was a strong swimmer, exceptionally fit, and had no fear of the water. Her father had been keen for her to swim from an early age; having been brought up by parents who both had phobias about water, Brendan Prince had been determined not to pass on the same fear to his children. It was only in later years she discovered he was still frightened of swimming when her mother revealed how he'd kept it hidden from her.

Rachel was much further out to sea now, swimming against larger waves. She wondered how far she could go without tiring. Just when she was debating whether to swim back towards the shore with the tide, she noticed something further out, floating in the water.

Paddling in a stationary pose, she jumped as high as she could with the next wave, trying to see what it was. Shocked to see a body being tossed about in the strong currents like a rag doll, disappearing under and then surfacing again, Rachel looked around, but there was no-one to call. She swam as fast and as hard as she could until her muscles screamed from the pain of the effort.

Rachel felt tired and weak from mounting wave after wave and fighting unpredictable undercurrents. Still, she battled on until she caught the woman, who was limp and face down, before another wave submerged her. Rachel managed to turn her over while keeping them both afloat. She was surprised to find it was Carol North.

Rachel held Carol tight, trying to judge the distance to the shore, but deciding she wouldn't get her back in time to save her. She had to administer mouth to mouth now.

Rachel used every ounce of strength gained from all her hours in the gym and miles of road running over the years. She hoisted the woman up while treading water. Pinching Carol's nose, she inhaled a huge breath before forcing air into the other woman's lungs.

After several minutes, when Rachel was near exhaustion, Carol North coughed, spluttering out some seawater as she did so. She gasped in air and coughed some more, looking disorientated. Carol was weak but breathing. Rachel held onto her, realising that while she'd been resuscitating, the sea had carried them further away from the shore and beyond the safety flags where the currents became nigh-on impossible to maintain any degree of control over.

For the first time in her life, Rachel felt powerless against the mighty ocean. Carol was barely conscious and unable to help in any way, but at least she wasn't fighting. Rachel floated on her back, supporting Carol's head, determined not to let go, while trying to conserve energy. The sun beat down on her own head and she gazed into the sky, imagining how broken Carlos would be without her.

Then she heard her father's voice in her head.

"When you're in the darkest place and the deepest distress, that's when you'll find it the hardest to stop fighting and pray; but pray you must, because underneath you are the everlasting arms."

Rachel didn't know whether she was hallucinating or dying, but she recognised her faith had taken a battering since she'd been dealing with the worst of humanity. By the time she had finally caught up with the serial killer who'd challenged her at every turn, she had stopped praying. Now she looked up to the heavens, feeling a deep inner peace which made her load lighter.

Rachel prayed first for forgiveness, and then for safety for her and Carol. Afterwards, she closed her eyes, still holding the other woman, but stopping her struggle underneath the water. By doing so, she allowed their bodies to become buoyant.

Moments later, Rachel heard an engine and saw, through the haze, a boat heading in their direction. As the lifeboat pulled up alongside her, a woman called out.

"Don't worry, mam. We'll have you out in no time."

First, she threw Rachel a lifebuoy, then she jumped into the water and took Carol from her, passing the weak woman to two men leaning over the side. They hauled Carol onto the boat.

"Your turn," the woman said. Rachel was just about able to assist the men to get her on board, and the woman leapt back into the boat seconds later.

The lifeguards gave most of their attention to Carol North. The men wrapped her in a blanket and helped her exhale the rest of the seawater.

"Is one of you Rachel? You're lucky your friend called us when she did, or we wouldn't have got here in time," the woman said.

"I'm Rachel," she said. "Did Sarah call you?"

"Yes," the woman replied. "She insisted you were in trouble. She said she just felt it. We're spiritual people in India, so we take such feelings seriously."

"Thank you," Rachel was speaking to the people in the boat, to Sarah and, of course, to God.

"What happened?" Carol was now sitting up, fully conscious.

"I found you in the water," said Rachel. "You tell me." She was still unsure about Carol North.

"I went for a swim. The next thing I remember is something hitting me." A trembling hand reached to the back of the head. One of the men examined Carol's head. Then he spoke in Hindi to the woman who had jumped in the water.

"He says there's a lump. You must have hit a rock. It can be dangerous if you stray close to the reef back there."

The boat pulled onto the shore where the crew jumped out and beached it. Sarah was pacing up and down.

"Rachel. Thank God!" She noticed Carol. "What's she doing here?"

"I'll tell you over lunch and a coffee. I'm starving."

"We should check you out first, mam. An ambulance is waiting," the female lifeguard said.

Rachel followed the crew, who carried Carol on a stretcher, to the waiting ambulance. Once she got the all clear, she made her way with Sarah to a beach café. Rachel almost fell into a seat; her muscles were still hurting, but now they felt like jelly.

Sarah handed her a bottle of water, almost throwing it her way. "Get that down you. I'll get us some hot drinks and food, and then you can explain why you can't even go for a swim without getting into danger." Sarah's eyes flashed with concerned anger.

"It wasn't my fault," Rachel said, but Sarah had already stomped to the bar. *At least she had the good sense to collect our things*, thought Rachel, looking at the bag Sarah had pretty much thrown at her along with the water.

Chapter 22

Once Sarah had eaten and calmed down, she felt less angry with Rachel for almost getting herself killed yet again. The shock of the previous evening's attack must have left her sensitive and more jumpy than usual. What Jason had revealed about members of the crew threatening to do her harm hadn't helped, leaving her with the impression of being betrayed.

Disappointment coursed through her veins. Everything she did was aimed at making life for passengers and crew better, from health check-ups to treatments. Now, it appeared there were those who would harm her to get to Jason. Sarah had been livid with him when he told her what he'd been hiding from her, shouting at him like she'd never done before for keeping secrets. In fairness to him, he had taken her anger and harsh words without retaliating, which in the end made her feel guilty. Then she had yelled at him again for not reacting. In the cold light of day, Sarah had seen sense and they had apologised to each other. Now this. What next?

"Why can't you just come on a cruise holiday and leave your job behind, Rachel?"

"Tell me, if you were staying with me and someone collapsed on the floor, would you leave them there?" Rachel retorted. She looked shattered and Sarah felt bad for being so angry with her, but she had been frantic with worry when she sensed something had happened to her friend. She had feared Carol North, or whoever Darrell's killer was, had tracked Rachel down and killed her, such was the weight that fell onto her stomach. Sarah had paced the beach carrying both their bags before finally grabbing a lifeguard and convincing him to send out a search boat. When she had seen Carol in the boat with her friend, she imagined her premonition had been right, but Rachel had come out on top.

"I guess not, but I would if there was a doctor around. As there's a security team on board the *Coral Queen,* so should you. What happened out there, Rachel? Did she try to kill you?"

"No. What happened today had nothing to do with me investigating anything. I saw someone in trouble – more than that, actually – and I went to help. It could have been anyone; I didn't know it was going to turn out to be Carol North. Truth be told, I'd rather it had been anyone other than her I brought back from near dead."

Rachel was hiding something from her, but Sarah didn't know what. "Is that because you think she killed Darrell? You really liked him, didn't you?" she asked.

Rachel sighed. "Can we do this some other time, Sarah? My legs and arms feel like jelly."

It wasn't like Rachel to admit to weakness. "Sorry. You did the right thing. Of course you did. I just hate the thought of everyone I know and love being in danger: you, Jason, Carlos…"

Her best friend's hand reached out for hers. "I understand, Sarah. It's eating away at me too, but somehow I have to believe that everything will turn out okay. Carlos will come home, Jason and I will go on catching bad guys, and you'll keep healing the sick. It's more than a job to us. It's what makes us tick. Besides, when I was out there today, I had a deeper sense of God's presence than I've ever known. Whether we live or die, this isn't where it ends. We just have to live the best lives we can and not be tainted by what baddies throw at us."

"You're right. We can't let anything come between us. I'll drink to that." Sarah held her mug up for Rachel to join her toast.

"Do you think they'll keep Carol North in hospital?" Rachel asked.

Sarah thought for a moment. "They might want to, but I don't know what the medics in India can do if she refuses. She looked fine to me, considering you say she'd not long since been near dead."

"Have you ever tried doing mouth to mouth in the water?"

"The advantage of being a nurse is I never have to do mouth to mouth at all. We have things called CPR pocket masks. I've got one in my handbag."

"Now she tells me." Rachel laughed, then scowled.

"I know that look, and don't give me the jelly legs excuse again. What is it you're not telling me?"

Rachel grinned at her, blue eyes lighting up. The food had clearly done her the world of good.

"My legs do feel like jelly."

"I believe you, and I'll gladly get you a massage when we get back to the ship, but there's nothing wrong with your mouth."

"For a nurse, you can be harsh sometimes."

Sarah folded her arms; she wasn't giving in this time. "I'm waiting."

Rachel took her time finishing her third strong black coffee as if mulling something over. Sarah was becoming impatient.

"I'm sick of people keeping things from me. I'm not made of jelly. Tell me what's bothering you."

Rachel lifted her eyes from the mug. There was a hint of sadness as she spoke.

"Carol North was wearing a ring. A distinctive looking ring with an unmistakeable shape. I—"

Sarah's hand automatically went to her right cheek. "You recognised it from the photos Bernard took last night. She was the one who attacked me. Somehow, I thought it was her once you told me what Gaz had said. You should have left her in the water." Sarah laughed but was disturbed by the news.

"Believe me, if I'd known, rather than suspected, I might have done."

"When did you know?"

"I had my suspicions, but I wasn't sure until we got here. I was having flashbacks and recalled seeing the ring in passing while the lifeboat crew were assessing and treating her. It didn't click then, but I remember it clearly now."

"What will happen if they keep her in hospital?" Sarah asked, half-hoping that's what would happen so this entire episode could be brought to a close.

"I suppose Waverley will call the police and have them interview her about Darrell, but there's no actual evidence and they might not do much about her thumping you. I've been debating whether to go over to the hospital and talk to her myself."

Sarah couldn't believe her ears. "You'll do no such thing. What have we been talking about for the past hour? You can be stone deaf when you want to be, Rachel Jacobi-Prince."

"Come on, Sarah. Wouldn't you like to know what was so important she had to get rid of it last night and why she would dare attack a ship's officer in that way? What if the Goan police just let her off with a caution, or worse, do nothing? We don't have any evidence she drugged or killed

Darrell, but I'm sure I can get her to talk. Sarah, I've decided. I'm going, with or without you."

"You can be so stubborn sometimes. Of course I'm coming." What Rachel had said made sense; she *did* want to know why Carol North hit her. "We haven't got long. We need to be back on board in two hours. Will your jelly legs and arms survive a quick dash to the hospital?"

They both burst out laughing.

***

Sarah had never been on the inside of an Indian hospital before. She hadn't worked in a British hospital for some time, but as soon as she and Rachel entered the bustling main entrance, she could see the difference. What was considered busy in the UK was nothing compared to this place.

Patients were lined up outside when they entered. Inside, the hospital was jam-packed and, at first glance, struck her as chaotic. As well as the familiar antiseptic smells, her nose twitched, struck by the odours of home-cooked food mingled with spices. Sarah tried to imagine nursing in this situation and resisted the urge to cover her ears with her hands to escape the noise.

Rachel was on a mission; not pausing for a moment, she headed straight to the reception where she was told to join a long queue. While Sarah would have loved to have rolled her sleeves up and given the local nurses a hand, Rachel was bemoaning the wait.

"This won't do," she said to Sarah. "We'll never get to see Carol before the ship sails at this rate. Where would they have taken her?"

"Casualty, I would have thought. If they've already moved her on, they should be able to tell us where to."

"Right," said Rachel, glancing around at the signs written in Konkani, the official language of Goa, Hindi and Portuguese. There were some English signs but none saying Casualty.

"We'd be better off going outside and watching for ambulances," suggested Sarah.

"Good idea." Rachel turned on her heel and frogmarched Sarah back the way they had come.

"There," said Sarah. "An emergency ambulance has gone that way." She watched it climb a hill and turn left.

"Come on," said Rachel, breaking into a jog. "Hurry."

I don't know what happened to the jelly legs, Sarah thought, trying to keep pace with her friend but falling behind.

"It's difficult jogging with my arm in a sling," she complained.

"Take it out then," Rachel called over her shoulder, not slowing now she was on a mission.

"Why did I have to choose a manic best friend?" Sarah muttered to herself while gingerly removing her arm from the sling. She tried to run, but every step tore at the cut on her face and sent throbbing pain through her right wrist.

"I can't do it, Rachel," she called but to no avail. Rachel had already turned the corner. "Thanks a bunch," Sarah yelled into the air. Slowing her pace and putting the arm back in the sling for comfort, she noticed a group of people waiting outside another building resembling a clinic. Her face broadened into a grin.

"Serves you right, Prince," she said out loud but fired off a text.

Sarah walked past the disjointed queue and joined Carol North, who was sitting on a bench outside the hospital.

"Hello," she said. "Remember me?"

"The one from the caves and didn't I see you on the beach earlier?" Carol's tone was wary although not unfriendly.

"Yes, you did. It was my friend who rescued you this afternoon. She'll be along in a minute. How are you feeling?"

"Fine. I've just told the doctor inside there, I'm not staying in that place."

"Are you sure that's wise?" Sarah asked.

"Look around you. These people need the space far more than I do. The pharmacist's just sorting out some antibiotics, then I can go. They're worried I might get pneumonia because I inhaled so much seawater."

Sarah nodded. "That makes sense." Rather than feel anger towards this woman, Sarah felt sorry for her, until she glanced down at the ring on her right hand and automatically reached for her cheek.

"Have you been in the wars as well?" Carol asked, nodding towards her arm. Sarah didn't have time to respond as Rachel arrived.

"There you are," she said to Sarah.

"Carol's being discharged with antibiotics," Sarah said. "She wondered if I'd been in for treatment."

Rachel's stare hardened. "Someone attacked my friend last night, as you well know," she said, not taking the usual subtle approach. Her eyes were piercing through Carol North's.

"What are you on about? How should I know? All I know is you two keep popping up all over the place like—"

"Luckily for you," said Rachel. "Or your body would have been washed up on some distant shore someday."

Carol dropped the resistance. "Thanks for that. I owe you. Let me know if there's any way I can repay you."

Rachel joined her on the newly vacated bench after an older couple were called into the building. "You can start by telling us what you threw over the side of the ship last night, and why you hit my friend here."

Carol turned on Rachel. Looking at her as if she'd taken leave of her senses, she then glanced at Sarah.

"Are you suggesting I did that?"

"Not just suggesting it; I know it," said Rachel.

"I don't know what you've been taking, but you've got it all wrong."

"And I suppose I'm wrong in believing you drugged Darrell in the restaurant the night he died?"

This time, Sarah noticed a glimpse of fear in Carol's eyes before she regained control.

"You're barking. Is your friend unhinged?" Carol addressed Sarah.

"Only when protecting those she loves." Sarah changed tack. "Nice ring you've got there."

"What? Yeah, thanks." Carol looked at the ring before glaring at Rachel. "Look, it's been a rather traumatic day without being accused of things I know nothing about, so if you don't mind, I'd like you to leave."

"Not until you tell me what went over the side," said Rachel. "You see, that ring has a lot of distinguishing features. It's unique, and it left an indentation on Sarah's face. You can't see the marks now, but we have photos back on board to prove it."

Carol's eyes widened. "Oh, my goodness! That's why she gave me the ring."

Sarah felt like she had brain fatigue all of a sudden as she fought off another flashback from the night before.

"Who? Who gave you the ring?"

"Sangita. She gave it to me this morning. I've been admiring it ever since we got here and asking her where I could get one like it. She told me it had been made to order, and there wasn't another like it. Then, this morning, out of the blue, she gave it to me. I couldn't believe my luck."

Sarah and Rachel exchanged glances. "Did you see much of Sangita last night?" Rachel asked.

"No. She cleared off about five minutes after Earl Spence left our meeting. Word is they're having a fling. Some people will do anything to get on in the world, but she won't get the job. I'm certain it's mine."

Carol's eyes widened, jaw dropping. Her hand rubbed the back of her head.

"Do you think someone could have thrown a rock at me this afternoon?"

Rachel looked thoughtful. "I don't know, but I think you should be careful who you trust until the security team finds out what happened to your colleague, Darrell Baker. If you really are next in line for the job, you could be in danger."

"Are you sure you wouldn't rather stay here?" Sarah asked.

"Absolutely." Carol stuck her chin forward, determination in her eyes. "I'm becoming paranoid, like your friend here. I hit my head on a rock like the lifeguard people said."

"We'll leave you to get on, then, until we bump into each other again," said Rachel, taking Sarah's good arm. "And I wouldn't be so sure about the promotion. From what I've heard, it's wide open."

"How will you get back to the ship?" Sarah asked.

"Taxi." Carol's snub-nosed face was doing its best to look down on Rachel, which simply made her look silly. Sarah was experiencing mixed emotions: happiness that Carol hadn't attacked her but fury towards Sangita.

"Do you think this afternoon was an accident?" she asked Rachel as they walked away from Carol.

"First the fall in the caves, now the rock." Rachel's eyes were set like steel. "I doubt it very much."

Chapter 23

Once back on board the ship, Rachel and Sarah passed through security. Rachel was on the lookout for Waverley, Jason or Rosemary, but none of them were on boarding duty. She recognised Ravanos, a security guard, and a few of the others from previous cruises, but no-one they could talk to.

Rachel suggested Sarah text Jason and let him know they needed to share the information they now had. Jason texted back that Waverley and Rosemary were in a meeting with Goan police officers, and he was on duty at the crew security entrance. He suggested they meet after dinner.

"Shame we can't gate-crash Waverley's meeting." Rachel was feeling impatient. They'd entered a lift and were on their way up to their respective decks.

"I'm quite pleased myself," said Sarah. "I'm worn out. I'd like a shower and a good meal after the day we've had.

Speaking of which, I still can't believe you ran off and left me to fend for myself back at the hospital."

Rachel had been feeling guilty about jogging ahead, realising how single-minded she could be when on a mission.

"We were under time pressure. Besides, I knew you'd stop. You're sensible like that."

"I hate to point it out to you, but you told me to lose the sling and keep up!"

"Did I?"

"You're exasperating, but I *was* sensible, unlike some." Sarah grinned. "Which, as it turns out, was a good thing or we might never have found Carol. How are the jelly legs and arms, by the way?"

Rachel winced, massaging her aching biceps. "Don't rub it in. You know as well as I you do what you have to do." Now, though, she longed to soak in a warm bath, but there wasn't one in her stateroom. "If Marjorie was on board, I'd use her bath instead of slumming it with a shower."

"My heart bleeds for you," said Sarah.

"I might grab a change of clothes and head up to the spa. Do you fancy coming?"

Sarah held up her plastered arm. "Doh!"

"Whoops, sorry. I'm not getting it right today, am I?"

"You were doing fine until you decided to take on the Indian Ocean. I'm pleased you managed to save that wretched woman, but I shudder to think what could have happened to you."

"Thanks to you, we don't have to go there." Rachel quipped, but she was certain she'd get flashbacks later.

The lift stopped at Sarah's floor. "I'll meet you in the buffet at seven-thirty. You get a soak in the jacuzzi or something; I need to get some rest."

Rachel wanted to remind her friend she had promised to get her a massage, but she'd put Sarah through enough for one day. A jacuzzi would work.

"Have a nap, I'll see you later."

Rachel went to the jacuzzi on deck fourteen, which was quieter than usual. Most passengers would still be boarding after their day in Goa and might even have had enough sun. Either that, or they were changing for dinner. She leaned back, closed her eyes and enjoyed the warmth of the water and the refreshing bubbles.

She must have been in the water for around ten minutes when she heard a familiar voice.

"Hey! I've been looking for you."

Rachel forced her eyelids to open. Gaz's dark blue eyes were staring down at her. He removed the towel from around his waist and got in, sitting opposite.

"Why?"

"I heard what happened to Carol and how you rescued her. It sounds incredibly daring, doing something like that. I'd have been hopeless. I'm not a great swimmer. You seem to have a habit of saving people."

Rachel thought back grimly to the first day of the cruise, when she had jumped in front of a fast-moving car to save Darrell, only to find she'd just delayed his demise. She hoped it wouldn't be the same for Carol North, not that she liked the woman.

On reflection, Rachel might have increased the likelihood of herself or Sarah becoming targets if word was spreading this fast. Her thoughts raced – she should have insisted Sangita be put under house arrest until she and Waverley had a chance to talk to her.

"Does everyone know what happened?"

"Pretty much. I'm not sure if Stoney knows about it yet, but I guess she will soon. Sorry to hear about your friend, the nurse. Stoney told us at this morning's meeting she'd been attacked or something. Apparently, she helped with some first aid."

"Thanks. Sarah's fine, and grateful to your boss. How was Carol when you saw her?"

"Spitting mad, actually. She was making all sorts of accusations about someone throwing a rock at her this afternoon. I think the saltwater's gone to her brain."

Selfish woman. Clearly she wasn't concerned about Sarah, Rachel thought. "Hang on. Did you say Dr Stone told you this morning about the attack on Sarah? Were you all there?"

Gaz nodded. "Yep. Why do you ask?"

"I was just wondering, that's all." Rachel paused. Why the heck had Carol North pretended not to know about it? Thoughts swirled around her brain.

"Carol's near-drowning might not have been an accident," she said. "The lifeguards examined a bump to her head; a rock had definitely hit her." Rachel didn't mention they thought it was most likely an accident.

"Blimey. Don't tell me someone's got it in for Carol now. If it carries on like this, I might end up getting the promotion after all."

Gaz laughed. Rachel raised an eyebrow.

"It puts paid to your theory Carol drugged Darrell, doesn't it?"

Gaz shrugged. "So we're back to a mugging."

"Seriously, do you think anyone among you is ruthless enough to remove the competition by any means?"

Gaz spread his arms over the back of the jacuzzi and stared at the setting sun. "Until this week, I didn't know any of these guys, but I can tell you one thing: I wouldn't want to be the one standing in their way if there is. Carol's unfeeling and uncaring. My money would have been on her, but then she nearly died today, so I guess that rules her out. Lizzie makes out she's a bit dizzy – Lizzie Longlegs, Darrell called her – but beneath all that pretence, she's got a heart of ice. Matt gives off the impression he only wants a good time, but I think he'd do pretty much anything to get one over on his family, who don't approve of his career choice."

"What about murder?" Rachel asked.

Gaz shook his head. "I'd say he's more the bribing or blackmailing type; he's keeping a pretty close eye on Sangita and Earl to that end."

"Do you think Sangita would kill to get to the top?"

"You know, I can't believe I'm saying this, but I think she might. If Lizzie's ice, she's liquid helium. Totally ignores me because I'm a lowly research scientist without the senior in front. She's also got the connections in India if you're thinking the car thing was a hire job. Darrell and her argued in the restaurant on the first night when she kept firing put-downs at him in front of Earl. That was when we were both still with it."

Rachel was amused at the liquid helium reference. There was more to Gaz than she had imagined.

"Go on... any other theories?"

"Well, if Earl was up for the promotion, I'd have included him, but as he has a say, it can't be. I might be biased because I don't like the guy. Sadly, his only vice is taking advantage of impressionable young women."

Rachel would hardly describe Sangita Regum as impressionable, but she parked that thought.

"What about Dr Pantoni?"

"Pearl? Nah. Everyone agrees she's got no chance of getting the promotion, even if she knocked out all the competition. Stoney doesn't like her. I don't know why or what, but the others say there's history between those two. Also, Pantoni's too pathetic to be a killer."

Don't underestimate the quiet woman, thought Rachel, not sure whether to feel sorry for or worried about Pearl Pantoni. "She can't be that pathetic, having got to the position she has, and she holds a doctorate. I take it none of the others have that level of education?"

"No, they don't, but education's not everything. Besides, she and Darrell had formed an alliance after being snubbed by the rest of us, so I can't see her wanting to harm him. Everyone thinks she had a crush on him. Plus, she's the only one, besides Earl and me, who didn't do drugs that night."

"What drugs did they do?" Rachel played the innocent.

"Matt told me he got hold of some weed and shared it around. He didn't offer me any, mind, not that I would have taken it. I had a cousin who nearly died from taking so-called recreational drugs. I think his was spiked. Speaking of recreational drugs – word is, Sangie carries some around in her handbag."

Rachel's interest was piqued. "What sort of drugs?"

"No idea. I just overheard Lizzie having a go at her about it; warning that if she got caught, she'd be fired."

"I see," said Rachel. "Why would Lizzie care whether Sangita was fired? I would have thought she'd be more likely to report her than warn her."

"Dunno. Those two have become pretty thick over the past couple of days. Maybe 'cos Sangie's in with Earl and her father's rich and influential. I think Stoney needs the Indian branch, but whether she'd tolerate drug use is another matter."

What a cold-hearted bunch of people. How on earth did one company attract so many like-minded psychopaths? Rachel thought.

"Hey, do you think Sangie might have been the one who spiked Darrell's drink that night?" Gaz asked. Rachel certainly did, but she was wondering what Gaz was up to. Was he watching his colleagues and trying to help her, or was he misdirecting and manipulating?

She checked her watch. "I'm sorry, I need to go. I'm meeting Sarah for dinner," she said.

"Blimey! Is that the time? We've got another meeting before dinner." Gaz rolled his eyes. "See you around, Rachel. Let's hope you don't have to save anyone else, but if you do, let it be me." He winked and jogged off, laughing.

Be careful what you wish for. Rachel had a sudden fear that Gaz might play amateur detective, and if he did, he had no idea how merciless this killer was. It was time to put that person away.

Chapter 24

Waverley appeared relaxed, almost smug, when he stood to welcome Rachel and Sarah into his office. Jason walked over and kissed Sarah, checking she was okay. They sat around Waverley's casual table where drinks had already been laid out.

"I took the liberty of ordering a martini and lemonade for Rachel and a white wine for you, Sarah. Jason suggested a Pernod might be too strong with the painkillers."

"Thanks," said both women, sharing a 'what's going on?' look.

"How was your interview with the Goan police?" Rachel asked. She had watched the uniformed officers leave before the ship left port.

"Fine. They reiterated Mr Baker was struck twice on the head with death occurring from a brain haemorrhage, something we already knew from the pathologist in Mumbai. Early toxicology reports showed traces of amphetamines in the dead man's system. They are happy for us to continue with our inquiries while the Mumbai police interview locals who are willing to help; they are keeping it a low-profile investigation unless the family kicks off. The police don't wish to damage the tourist industry unnecessarily—"

"Heaven forbid," Rachel interrupted, drawing a frown from Waverley.

"As I was saying, they've kept the death out of the newspapers."

Rachel felt a kick from Sarah, so she held her peace.

"We can now share some good news. The police gave us some useful information, plus we have found evidence and believe we know who drugged Mr Baker." Waverley helped himself to a self-congratulatory sip of Scotch.

"Sangita Regum," said Rachel.

Waverley frowned, his bubble burst. "How did you know that?"

Rachel noticed Sarah's brows puckering. "We gathered some information ourselves this afternoon. Do go on, Chief."

Waverley proceeded with less enthusiasm. "We found a bottle of pills on deck fifteen, below where your attacker struck, Sarah."

"But I looked there this morning," said Rachel. "I couldn't find anything."

"Neither did we until Inglis noticed a broken grille and got maintenance to remove it. A bottle of tablets had lodged itself in a hole too small for it to fall down, otherwise we'd never have found it."

"Are you certain it belongs to Sangita?" Sarah asked.

"Several witnesses from the restaurant, including staff, reported seeing a pill bottle sticking out of her handbag on the night in question. It appears Miss Regum's arrogance knows no bounds. She believes that because she is well known – or rather, her father is – in Mumbai, she's untouchable.

"That's another reason the police have left any further action to us. They can't prove her guilty of murder and don't want to make an enemy of Mr Regum. As the sergeant told us this afternoon, he's likely to contact their superiors and have them demoted to traffic."

"They're right, though," said Rachel. "Even if you have the drugs tested and they turn out to be the same as those in Darrell's system, she could say he took them with consent, so it doesn't prove her guilty of anything."

Waverley brushed back his imaginary hair. "That may be, but we can remove her from this ship. We don't allow drug use, and we certainly do not let passengers get away with assaulting a ship's officer. If I'd had the drugs earlier, I'd have thrown her off in Goa."

"It was Sangita who attacked Sarah, that we know," said Rachel, explaining what had happened during the afternoon. She brushed off questions about the traumatic sea rescue and hurried to the point where they had quizzed Carol North about the ring. "Sangita gave it to Carol this morning. I assume she did so after finding out from her boss who it was that had been attacked last night. It was a silly mistake. If I'd been her, I'd have thrown it in the sea. Giving it to Carol North doesn't make sense unless, of course, she had also determined to kill Carol."

"Ah yes," said Jason, "knowing we'd pull the information together and conclude that Miss North killed Darrell and couldn't live with herself, or had a tragic accident. It would have been an ingenious plan if it had worked. The only problem is, with the scanty evidence we've got, all we can do is throw her off the ship."

"Far better than leaving her onboard and letting her kill anyone else," said Waverley. "Whether Dr Stone will fire her, in view of the girl's influential father, is a matter for her to decide."

"And Earl Spence," said Rachel.

"What's he got to do with it?" Jason asked.

"As well as being the head of PR, according to those I… er… we've spoken to, he and Sangita have been having secret liaisons."

"So they *are* having an affair?" Waverley quizzed.

"That's the assumption. If so, he might persuade Dr Stone to be lenient in view of the lack of evidence for murder. When can we talk to her?"

"'We' won't be talking to her." Waverley gestured his hand between Rachel and himself. "Inglis and I will interview her…" he checked his watch "… in half an hour. I've asked Inglis to escort her to her stateroom. She will be under house arrest until we arrive in Kochi the day after tomorrow."

Rachel stared at Waverley. "There's something not right here."

"You've just said yourself she was the one who attacked Sarah, and we have the drugs."

"True. But what if Carol North's story is fake?"

"What do you mean, Rachel?" Sarah asked.

Rachel screwed up her eyes, trying to think. "Something's been bothering me. According to Gaz – I met him when I went upstairs to unwind in the jacuzzi – Dr Stone told all the pharma team this morning about Sarah's attack. But when we spoke to Carol this afternoon, she pretended not to know anything about it. Why would she do that unless she had something to do with it?"

"Rachel's right," said Sarah. "Carol made a big thing of asking me if I'd been getting treatment at the hospital, commenting that I looked like I'd been in the wars as well."

"Why the pretence?" Rachel asked.

Waverley sighed, confused. "But they are Miss Regum's drugs we've found, and the witnesses from the restaurant concur. The lady is well known there."

"Drugs on open display in her handbag," said Jason. "Anyone could have removed the bottle, administered a couple to Darrell, and then tried to get rid of them last night."

"Or," said Rachel, "what if the person wanted to be seen throwing something over the side? They waited for the right moment when a member of the crew would walk by, assuming they'd be challenged for littering the ocean.

The plan was to hit the officer before going down to the next deck, looking for a suitable place to hide the drugs."

"They could even have found the hiding place first, then come up to the next deck to execute their plan," suggested Jason.

"Isn't this all a bit farfetched?" Waverley looked incredulous.

"Farfetched but clever," said Rachel.

"But what about the ring?" Sarah asked. "Surely the rest of the group would know whose it was."

"That's where we caught her," said Rachel. "She had to think fast this afternoon and most likely made up that story about Sangita having given her the ring on the hoof. She's counting on two things, the first being that her colleagues are such a bunch of narcissists that none of them would recall who wears what. The second is an assumption that we would report Sangita to security and leave you to take it from there, Chief Waverley. She probably hoped the drugs would colour your thinking enough for you to ignore anything else Regum tells you. She doesn't know you're married to a security officer, Sarah."

"So it's Miss North we need to speak to?" Waverley marched over to his desk and picked up his radio. "Inglis, let Miss Regum go. Bring Miss North to my office. Now."

"Yes, sir." Rosemary's confusion was clear in her voice. "Just to clarify, you want me to release Miss Regum from house arrest and bring Miss North to you?"

"Correct."

"Let me and Sarah stay now," said Rachel.

"Very well. We'll see what pack of lies she conjures up next, shall we?"

**

Instead of being afraid when she set eyes on Rachel and Sarah, Carol appeared relieved.

"Please take a seat, Miss North." Waverley indicated a vacant chair around the table. "I'm Chief Waverley. You may know I head up security on this ship. You've already met Officer Inglis, Officer Bradshaw and Rachel here. This is Officer Goodridge, another member of the security team. We'd like to ask you a few questions."

"About this afternoon? They told you about the attack on me?"

Carol North was playing it cool, so cool. Waverley seemed unsure of himself for a brief moment, but he recovered quickly.

"Indeed. But I want to talk about the attack on Officer Bradshaw here. I believe you are wearing the exact same ring that left an indent in her face during an unprovoked attack last night. Here are the photographs."

Waverley laid a few images on the table in front of Carol, tapping them to point out the indentation. Carol appeared less sure of herself now. She glared at the two friends, Rachel in particular.

"I've already explained the ring isn't mine. It belongs to Sangita."

"I'd rather not play games, Miss North. The thing is, I don't believe you. We found these on the deck below where Nurse Bradshaw and her assailant – you – were standing last night."

Waverley laid the bottle of pills on the table next to the photos. Carol's eyes betrayed her.

"You've seen these before," said Rachel. "These are the tablets you pretended to throw overboard last night."

With flashing eyes, Carol turned on Rachel. "Yes, I've seen them before; they belong to Sangita. Why are you questioning me rather than her? I didn't hit your nurse. Believe it or not, I don't go around hitting people."

"But you do drug them," said Waverley.

Carol stared at the chief, indignation replaced by fear. "What do you mean?"

"We have seen CCTV footage of you slipping pills into Darrell Baker's drink in the O Pedro restaurant on the night he was killed," Rachel said.

Ignoring the gawps from the others, Rachel kept her eyes on Carol. It worked. The obstinate woman was ready to cave in.

With trembling lips, voice shaking, Carol said, "I drugged him, but I didn't kill him." She looked down at her hands.

"Why should we believe you?" Waverley pressed, shaking his head at Rachel.

"Because I'm telling the truth. A group of us met Sangita the night before we were due to board the ship. She bragged about the high pills she took when she wanted to stay awake; how they improved her performance. To be honest, I wasn't even sure I believed her, assuming it was her youth trying to impress.

"Then, when we were out for dinner, Darrell kept sniping at me about how he'd get the promotion and I should just accept it. He was getting on my nerves. The guy was unbearable enough without giving him any more power. I had to stop him.

"It was while the rest were messing around playing some silly game, I spied the bottle at the top of Sangita's open handbag." She paused before looking up at Rachel. "I'm not proud of it, but I took a couple and dunked them in a cocktail some tourist had left at the bar. I was having second thoughts when Darrell came to the bar and started again. That's when I shoved the cocktail in his direction and told him he was enough to put anyone off their drink. He picked it up and supped on the straw, mocking like.

"Ten minutes later, he was high as a kite, but he became aggressive with it. He was an embarrassment, and once Dr Stone came in, I could see she wasn't impressed."

"But you weren't sure she would hold it against him, so you finished him off outside the nightclub." Waverley's tone was severe.

Carol's eyes widened. "No. I'm telling you, I didn't kill him. Why would I? I could tell from Earl's reaction – Earl detested him – that Darrell wouldn't get the job."

Waverley ignored her protests. "And finding yourself still in possession of the pills, or maybe stealing them again later, you decided to frame Sangita Regum and put her out of the running for this sought-after promotion."

"No, I'm telling you! That's all I did. I felt bad about it, but figured some local had robbed Darrell that night. Regarding the ring and everything, I'm telling the truth. It belongs to Sangita."

"If that's the case, why did you pretend you didn't know Sarah – Nurse Bradshaw – had been attacked last night when Dr Stone told you all in your early morning meeting?" Rachel challenged.

"What? She didn't; at least, not while I was there. I was late. She might have said something before I came in. It was after the meeting Sangita gave me the ring. I think she might have been the one who threw the rock at me from the reef."

"I've heard enough of this nonsense," said Waverley. "We will hold you in the ship's brig until we arrive in Kochi, where we'll hand you over to the local police and you can tell them your fanciful story."

Shock and disbelief filled Carol's wild eyes as angry tears ran down her face. "You're wrong about this. I'm innocent. I didn't attack you," she appealed to Sarah. "You saw the lump on my head," she tried Rachel. "You can't think that was an accident, not when you take everything else into account."

"Take her to the brig, Inglis," Waverley ordered.

After Inglis and Carol left the room, Waverley was chipper. "I'd say that wraps this thing up, wouldn't you? Now, I'd like an early finish for once, so if you'll excuse me, I'll bid you goodnight. Sleep well, ladies. At least you can work knowing your wife isn't in danger, Goodridge."

"Yes, sir. I'll see you later." Jason kissed Sarah before heading out.

Rachel and Sarah left the chief's office at the same time and took the lift. When Sarah got out, she kissed Rachel on the cheek.

"Goodnight, Rachel. By the way, that's called deception, but thanks."

Rachel forced a smile. "I couldn't get away with it in the day job." She walked back to her stateroom with a heavy heart. Could it be she had directed Waverley to arrest the wrong person?

Chapter 25

It was around 3am when Rachel gave up trying to sleep. She pulled her shorts and a t-shirt on and headed down to the security hub, hoping Jason would be on his own.

He unlocked the security door and stood back, letting her through.

"You don't seem surprised to see me," she said.

"I suspect you have the same doubts I do. Either our probable perp gave a very convincing performance, or she's only guilty of what she says she is."

"How can we find out if she's telling the truth? Have you asked Sangita about the ring?"

"First thing I did. She admits it was her ring but says she gave it to Carol North yesterday morning; or should I say, two mornings ago, in view of the hour? So before the attack on Sarah."

"What did she say about the drugs?"

"She admits to taking recreational drugs but denies having any on board. I guess she's scared to admit she brought them onto the ship in case we charge her. I didn't mention the witness statements from the restaurant."

"We know from Carol's testimony, the statements, and from what Gaz told me, she's lying about that. I wonder if Gaz would have noticed when the ring switched hands. He's pretty astute," said Rachel. "Although, even if Sangita did try to get rid of the drugs and wallop Sarah, Carol's still the standout suspect for Darrell's murder. It's so frustrating. We must be missing something."

Rachel glanced around the room. There were monitors where cameras recorded various parts of the ship on a continuous loop. The only one switched on was that over the casino. Jason was clearly checking that the gambling syndicate hadn't found a new leader after the ejection of Mr Maku. A board on the wall, similar to the crime scene board she used at work, listed cases currently under investigation. Darrell's name and photo were at the top of one column, Maku's heading another.

Jason caught her eye. "Nice one about the CCTV footage, by the way. I don't know what we'd have done if she'd denied it."

Rachel grinned. "Has she signed a statement?"

"Inglis got her to write out her story, and that's what she's signed. She's still adamant she didn't kill Baker, and that she didn't attack Sarah."

"I'm inclined to believe her on the latter. She'll deny the former unless we can gather enough evidence to prove her guilty – or innocent – and I'm afraid that's unlikely with the trail going ever colder. She has a point that she'd more than likely achieved her goal. Even Gaz says Darrell had blown it long before they arrived at the nightclub."

"So we're back to a local mugging," said Jason.

"Or a more sinister motive."

"Like what?"

"That I don't know, but I intend to find out."

"I know that look," said Jason. "Should I be worried?"

"Has Darrell's phone turned up? Have you requested a call record?"

"The chief asked the police sergeant today to see what he could do. They have to request international cooperation, but as it's a murder inquiry, it should be granted."

"That'll take too long. Leave it with me. I'll make a few calls and see what I can do. What else have we got?"

"Not much. I've gone over and over the nightclub CCTV footage. I'm waiting for an old mate who's trying to find something from surrounding shops and so on. So far, most of the cameras have turned out to be deterrent fakes, but I haven't called her off in case she comes up with evidence to help convict Carol North."

"Or otherwise," said Rachel. "Haven't the Mumbai police looked into all this?"

"Not in the way Rosa will. She's relentless."

"Sounds like a good friend to have," said Rachel.

"We served together. She was a good soldier – took some flak, like all the female soldiers did, but she was totally dependable in a firefight."

Jason had never talked much to Rachel about his time in Afghanistan. He and Carlos had been in the army at around the same time, but their paths had never crossed. They'd done different tours. She knew they talked to each other in a way that only ex-servicemen and women can.

"What's Rosa doing in Mumbai?"

"Private security. It's where a lot of ex-squaddies go; either that, or they sell their skills to the highest bidder and become mercenaries."

"I've heard Carlos mention that." She didn't want to bring up the mental health issues many ex-soldiers developed, knowing that both Jason and Carlos still had their own struggles in that department.

"If there's anything to find, Rosa will find it, but whether we get anything before a killer walks off this ship free I can't guarantee."

"You don't think Carol killed Darrell, do you?"

Jason shrugged. "I'm keeping an open mind, but as you say, there doesn't seem to have been the need. Why kill him when she'd done what she set out to?"

"What are you going to do about Sangita?"

"I was just going through as much video footage of the day she says she gave the ring to Carol as I can. Do you want to help?"

"Why not?" said Rachel. "Sleep's overrated. I saw her on the afternoon in question, swimming in the pool and taking a jacuzzi with Lizzie Meeton. That was about threeish."

"Brilliant. Let's start there. We don't film the pool or we'd be accused of intrusive surveillance, but we film the deck edges in case anyone goes overboard."

Rachel and Jason spent the next two hours trawling through video, but it was useless. People had to hang over the rails to show up on camera and, if that were the case, they'd probably be throwing themselves over.

"Nothing," said Jason. "I think the best bet is going to be asking your Gaz and the others if they can help. From what you say, I don't hold much hope. They're all so self-absorbed, I doubt they'll remember who was wearing the ring and when."

"Hang on. What about the meeting rooms? Gaz said they had a meeting that night before they went their separate ways, not long before the assault on Sarah."

"That's better. We have cameras outside the purser's office to prevent theft; our main meeting room is just opposite. I'll pull up the film."

Jason spent a while tapping keys on a computer and going through various security protocols.

"Any idea what time they left?" he asked.

"No, but Sarah was called to her patient at nine-thirty. Try the two hours before that."

Before long, they had the right video, picking up passengers in the vicinity of the purser's office. Jason and Rachel checked the same screen.

"It's boring but might be worth it," said Jason.

"I'm going to be careful not to scratch my nose when I go near there in future."

"You're safe. We only pull these if a crime's been committed or like in this case, to help with inquiries."

The first hour yielded nothing. At around eight-thirty, Rachel saw Gaz's distinctive hair.

"Stop. That's Gaz. Go slowly, we might see the others." A few of the others paused to have brief conversations as they emerged from the meeting room, then moved away. Tia Stone said goodnight to someone out of the shot, and then Earl, who had left five minutes before, returned. A couple of minutes later, Sangita appeared and the two of them huddled together, having an intense conversation.

Jason paused the video. He zoomed in on her left hand.

"Nothing on the left." Jason allowed the footage to move slowly forward.

"Turn around," Rachel willed the woman.

The conversation ended, and Sangita made to walk away, Earl going in the opposite direction. She went out of the shot. Jason sat back in his chair.

"Blast."

"Hang on," said Rachel. "She's come back. Now."

Jason paused the video and zoomed in.

"Bingo!"

Chapter 26

After the lengthy session with Jason, Rachel had gone back to bed. They'd agreed to meet again once he'd discussed their findings and the next steps with Waverley. The chief wouldn't be happy to hear his neatly wrapped investigation had hit some turbulence, so she was glad it was Jason having to face his wrath.

Even after a refreshing shower, Rachel's eyes felt gritty, as though someone had rubbed sandpaper into them while she slept – or didn't. She suffered flashbacks from her exhausting rescue mission the day before, and now her arms and legs were yelping with pain as the aftereffects made their presence felt. As fit as she was, that near-death swim had sapped her energy, both mentally and physically.

She thought about Carol North and her story. Carol had been telling the truth about the ring, but what about the murder? Rachel hoped Jason and Waverley would interview Sangita themselves, or better still, Waverley and

Rosemary, because if they involved Rachel, she might be tempted to give the young woman a taste of her own medicine. The woman's arrogant attitude and brazen lies infuriated her. Sangita had hit Sarah and left her in agony with no thought of the consequences. Rachel found her coldness as repugnant as the assault. Sangita Regum was clearly ruthless enough to swat opposition out of the way without remorse. Perhaps she was the one who had killed Darrell.

With various scenarios spinning round in her head, Rachel stomped upstairs to the buffet. It had stopped serving breakfasts, but she grabbed a bread roll and a croissant from a lone tray. She took them outside, throwing herself down on a lounger. Overwhelmed was not something she was used to feeling, but that's how she felt now.

She closed her eyes tight, trying to force unwelcome thoughts from her mind. It was time to take a step back, before her emotions got the better of her. Rage was threatening to take over, which might make her do something she would later regret.

It wasn't Sangita Regum who was causing her so much distress; it was the constant fear that Carlos and Helena could disappear or be arrested in China. Then there was the unbidden and unspoken dread that Carlos might find the beautiful goddess impossible to resist while they were playing man and wife. Rachel rubbed her tired eyes aggressively – she couldn't let herself go down that road.

"I've been looking for you everywhere."

The welcome and soothing tone of her best friend brought Rachel back to the present.

"I slept in," she replied.

Sarah sat on the edge of her lounger. "You're crying. What is it?"

Rachel shook her head, angry with herself for being weak. She looked into the eyes of her concerned friend.

"I'm tired."

Sarah took her hand. "You're worried about Carlos."

All Rachel could do was nod. If she tried to say anything more, she would lose control.

"You haven't touched your food," Sarah scolded. "I bet you haven't had a proper breakfast, have you?"

"The food's stale. I was up half the night with your husband."

"It's not every woman who could say that to me and get away with it." Sarah laughed. Rachel found it impossible not to join in and, before long, they were both cackling hysterically.

Once they calmed down, Rachel held Sarah's gaze. "It was Sangita who attacked you."

"I know. Jason popped by and brought me breakfast in bed before he went to break the news to Waverley. I suppose Carol North still killed Darrell, though. It's a shame. I was beginning to like her, particularly after finding out she didn't thump me."

"I'm not sure there's much to like about any of them, apart from Gaz and your Matt."

"Perhaps like isn't the word. I feel sorry for her. I blame their boss for putting them under so much pressure. And, for your information, he's not *my* Matt."

"I wondered when you'd realise what I'd said." Rachel was feeling much better. It was good to talk about something else. "Nobody makes people do what they do. Although Dr Tia Stone seems to have created a toxic environment where vultures thrive."

Sarah moved to the edge of the lounger next to Rachel's. "I can't work her out. One minute she's like Cruella de Vil, and the next she's administering first aid to me like Florence Nightingale."

"Even the worst people can have a softer side," said Rachel. "I wonder what she makes of Carol's predicament... and soon she'll have to face Sangita's."

"She's not happy. Graham met with her again early this morning – they had prearranged a meeting after he ducked out of dinner the other night. She's seriously worried about the company's reputation. Someone has leaked information about Darrell's death, along with gossip about the vitriol amongst the senior scientists, to the board. They're considering bailing out."

"In what way?"

"I didn't ask, but I assume they want to disassociate themselves from what's going on. I guess they could ask the CEO to step down."

"Or sack their senior scientists, which would be rather radical," said Rachel.

"Perhaps they'll let the company take a buyout," suggested Sarah.

"Mm," said Rachel. "Although I can't see Tia Stone going down easily, can you?"

"I would have agreed with you, but Graham said she looked devastated. If she's taking the blame for what's going on within the team, she might not have a choice."

"It seems harsh when she built the company up from nothing."

"But when you bring in a board of directors, you're accountable no matter who you are. And, let's face it, she's the one who put them in this winner-takes-all situation. It would have made more sense to proceed with the original team-building plan if you ask me."

"You're right. I was almost feeling sorry for Dr Stone. But whatever the circumstances, or whoever created them, there's no excuse for someone among this ambitious crew to become a predator. Who would want to work in that kind of environment anyway?"

"Strictly speaking, they don't work together in the true sense of the word, but I take your point," said Sarah.

"You're right, though, Sarah. If I was the one managing the company, I'd want to fix the relationships, so why did Tia Stone change her mind in the first place and make things worse? It seems counterproductive to me."

"What if the decision didn't come from her? Perhaps it was the board that wasn't keen on her promotion choice for some reason."

Rachel felt there was something in what Sarah was saying, but the sparks in her head just weren't coming together.

"I think you might be onto something, but boards rarely interfere in the day-to-day running of a company. I've learned that much from Marjorie."

Sarah shrugged. "If it was the case, and I might be wrong, it could be because somebody raised their concerns behind Tia's back. The same person who leaked Darrell's murder and what's happening in the team, I suspect."

Chapter 27

Sarah encouraged Rachel to go back to bed after lunch. Her friend must have been tired because she didn't put up any resistance.

"I'm worried about her," she told Jason after returning to their room. He had radioed her to tell her he was awake.

"Why?" He rubbed sleep from his eyes while she made him a second cup of tea, becoming quite adept at using her left hand.

"It's this whole Carlos thing, although I have to say, I'd be the same if it was you gallivanting undercover in China. Not to mention the drop-dead gorgeous Helena."

"I hardly think 'gallivanting' and 'undercover in China' go together." Jason pulled her into his arms, planting a kiss on her forehead. He brushed the back of his hand over her damaged cheek. "How is it?"

"It feels much better. Don't change the subject, Jason. Rachel's vulnerable at the minute; she needs rest, and I'm concerned her throwing herself into this Darrell thing is doing more harm than good, what with that and the kamikaze rescue things on day one and yesterday. If the lifeboat hadn't left when it did, she might have been dead." Sarah leaned in and rested her head on Jason's muscular shoulder. She always felt safe in his arms, and now the reason for his possessiveness was out in the open, the clouds hanging over them had evaporated.

"But it did get there, thanks to you. She's strong, Sarah. That reminds me: I said I'd let her know the outcome after I'd spoken with the boss."

Sarah lifted her head, glaring at him. "Have you heard a word I've just said?" Then she noticed the twinkling eyes. She hit him on the chest. "Don't tease."

"If it helps, I won't say anything. I'll let you tell her." Jason frowned. "Although neither of you will be happy with the outcome."

"Don't tell me: Sangita denies it after all that."

"Nope. She's admitted it. I wasn't there because of personal involvement and all that. According to the boss, she's apologised."

"That doesn't sound so bad."

"It's the next bit I don't like, and neither will you." Jason scowled even more deeply. "Anyone else and the boss would have expelled them tomorrow."

"Please don't say he's letting her off?" said Sarah, barely able to comprehend it. An attack on a ship's officer was tantamount to treason under normal circumstances.

"We already knew, but it appears her father is a *very* influential man. The boss put her under house arrest. As soon as his back was turned, she made a call. Her father called the cruise line. Apparently, he knows some people high up; they in turn called the captain. The sum of it is that she's mortified for her mistake, admits to having had too much to drink and lashing out without thinking. Her father, of course, is terribly sorry for your injuries and after asking what he could do to help the medical team, he's agreed to donate the onboard ultrasound scanner Graham has been fighting for."

"Blimey! That's a double-edged sword for Graham. He'll be thrilled to get the scanner but mortified at the cost to one of his team."

"You've just about summed up how he reacted when the boss broke the news. Not just that; this Mr Regum doesn't do small. He's donating a substantial sum of money to the Seafarers' Charity and has promised his daughter's behaviour will be impeccable for the rest of the voyage. I believe she wants to – or has been told to – personally apologise to you." Jason's voice dripped with sarcasm.

"That's something to look forward to. Rachel doesn't believe her capable of remorse, but it will be nice to witness the forced apology."

"You don't sound too cut up about it," said Jason.

"I'm not vindictive, Jason. You know that. As long as there's no more trouble from Rejuvenescence Pharma or its employees, I'll be happy."

"I hope Rachel responds with the same benevolence." He stroked her hair.

"She's got enough to worry about. Rachel can be philosophical about things when she needs to be. What about you?"

"I'm just happy that Maku isn't around anymore. I can live with having Sangita Regum aboard, especially if she's on her best behaviour. As long as you're okay with it, I am."

"What about Carol North?"

"She stays where she is. The boss won't budge on that issue, although I don't think he believes she murdered Darrell Baker any more than I do."

"Who did then?" Sarah asked.

"I guess it was some opportunist thief who saw the state he was in and robbed him for the dollars in his pocket and a phone. We still haven't been able to trace the phone; the sim will have been swapped over by now, and we have no access to Indian police records. Rachel said she was going to see if she could contact someone in the UK to get a copy of his phone records."

It was Sarah's turn to frown. "Well, let's hope she's forgotten about that and takes some time to switch off. I'm going to have words with Carlos when I see him again."

Jason put a hand behind his head, grinning at her. "Oh dear. Beware, Carlos."

She tried not to laugh but gave in. They lay in each other's arms for some time before Jason moved.

"I'd like to stay here forever, but I have to get back to work."

"You could tell the chief you've got a sick wife to look after," Sarah said, chuckling.

"I'd like to, but she's got a healthy left hook. Look at the bruise on my chest."

"Where?" Sarah was mortified, but he'd got her again. It was wonderful having her fun-loving, albeit tired, husband back. "Get to work before you drive me crazy," she teased.

"Aye, aye, Mrs; Officer Goodridge on his way." Jason headed towards the door in his underpants, making her shriek with laughter.

"I'd love to see Waverley's face if you went to work like that."

"Okay. If the lady can bear to be with me for a little longer, I'll take a shower."

Sarah threw a pillow at the shower room door as it closed behind him. She was tempted to join him, but she didn't want him to be late for work, not to mention the plaster on her right arm. It was hard being off duty when she felt so well.

She called through the door. "I'm going to see if Rachel's awake and get her to come for an early dinner. She didn't eat much earlier."

"Forever the nurse," he called back. "I finish at eleven."

"I'll be waiting," she said.

Sarah was smiling all the way down the corridor. All was well with her world again, and nothing could spoil it.

Chapter 28

Rachel had just got out of the shower when she heard a knock at the door. Sarah was standing there, looking radiant; Rachel was pleased things between her and Jason had clearly settled down.

"Thanks for persuading me to get a nap. I feel much better now," Rachel said.

"I'm pleased. Although you might not be so happy when I tell you the latest news."

"I expect I'm going to need a drink." Rachel opened a bottle of wine, pouring them a glass each. She then listened carefully while she got dressed. Sarah was telling her that Sangita Regum was going to get off with a warning for the assault because her father knew people and had somehow managed to bribe the cruise line.

"No wonder that girl gives the impression of being so untouchable," Rachel said. "I hope what he's donating costs a fortune." She checked her friend's face for stress, but Sarah still looked happier than she had all cruise.

"The ultrasound scanner Graham was after costs around eighty thousand dollars. Plus, he's giving a substantial sum to the cruise line's favoured charity."

Rachel whistled. "Boy, he really is wealthy. Why is it rich men can bribe their way out of trouble? In my opinion, he'd serve his daughter better by letting her take the punishment she deserves, not by bailing her out."

"I suppose that's how he operates. As you say, she oozes privilege and entitlement. The only good thing, although we'll all be pleased to have the scanner, is she's going to apologise to me personally."

"I'm surprised she's not sending a minion to do it on her behalf." Rachel huffed, feeling annoyed that Sangita Regum wouldn't be taught a harsh lesson. "You should record it for posterity. I bet she's not had to say sorry many times in her pampered life. How does Jason feel about it?"

"Resigned. But it's all right, Rachel. As I told Jason, I don't need revenge."

"No. But you do deserve justice," said Rachel.

"Speaking of justice, Waverley still plans to get rid of Carol North in the morning."

"It's a shame she doesn't have a rich father or mother. The woman was stupid for drugging Darrell, but I just can't see her killing him. Whereas I don't think Sangita would bat one of her very long eyelashes." Rachel was torn between letting Waverley make his own mistakes and the thing that drove her deep down inside, the thing Sarah wasn't recognising: justice. People couldn't go around the world thinking they could take another person's life. Rachel had committed her life to making sure such people were arrested and punished. Could she live with herself if she didn't pursue Darrell's murderer?

The answer came to her as she looked in the mirror, brushing her hair.

"You're not finished, are you?" Sarah asked.

"Yep, I'm ready. Let's eat."

"That's not what I mean, and you know it."

"Either way, we need to eat. Are you coming?"

Rachel didn't want Sarah worrying about her, and she certainly didn't want to put her in any further danger. If Sangita Regum was as savage as Rachel believed, she wouldn't hesitate to get rid of anyone standing in her way. The woman was a psychopath.

Rachel felt she had put a dampener on her friend's joy, so she did her best to counter it by suggesting they go for another steak. Sarah remained quiet over dinner. Rachel had cut the ribeye up for her, but she was picking.

Finally, she looked Rachel in the eye.

"Promise me you won't do anything stupid."

"I promise."

"And you'll let me help. If someone else killed Darrell, and that person attacked Carol, I want to have a hand in catching them."

"Absolutely not! Look at you, Sarah. You've only got one arm. Besides, Jason would never forgive me."

"I've seen you argue this out with Waverley frequently, Rachel, and I'm telling you now. It's not up to you. I get involved, with or without you."

A knot of fear found its way into Rachel's gut. She had never seen Sarah so serious.

"Okay. You win, but background stuff; no putting yourself in harm's way."

Sarah lifted a glass of white wine to her lips. "Agreed, Partner."

"And you have to tell Jason everything you're doing."

Sarah's forehead creased. "He'll be angry."

"Yep, but no more secrets. Isn't that what the two of you agreed?"

Sarah nodded. "You're right. I have to tell him, but if you think he's going to stop me, you're wrong. I'm not a child."

Rachel wished she had lied to Sarah and told her she would forget about it, but she couldn't do that. She was, however, determined to sort this out before Sarah had any opportunity to do anything that would put her in danger.

"If you're happy to skip dessert, I think I'd like to call it a day. I'm still tired from yesterday and my all-nighter," Rachel said as soon as Sarah had finished her steak, hoping she wasn't being too obvious.

"That's fine. Jason finishes in a couple of hours anyway, and I promised I'd be there. He's whacked out. The shifts are horrendous on this vessel."

"It's as bad as being a detective." Rachel laughed. "Other than when I'm cruising, I can't remember the last time I had a full weekend off. Crime in Leicester is incessant."

"You said you recently caught a serial killer. Was that awful?"

Rachel flicked the switch, blocking out the emotions from the case in the way she had done since she and her colleagues finally caught the perpetrator.

"It's something I have to forget, Sarah. I just can't talk about it."

"Sorry," said Sarah. "Perhaps it really is time to go to bed, otherwise you're going to need one of Bernard's Stingers."

Rachel laughed. "One day I'm going to have to try this infamous drink and judge for myself."

"Just make sure you've got a good supply of antacids and paracetamol at hand when you do."

The two women left the restaurant and headed to the lifts. They hugged when Sarah left the lift, and then Rachel headed up to her room to make some phone calls.

***

It proved impossible to get a record of Darrell Baker's phone log because it was registered to a US service provider. Rachel slapped her head.

"Idiot! Of course he would register it in America. What were you thinking?" She had to accept that this line of inquiry was a dead end and move on to something else.

Rachel paced the entertainment decks, wandering from bar to bar, hoping to find Gaz. She had just decided he must be having an early night when she spotted him in the Cigar Lounge – not the place she would have thought to search. Thankfully, he saw her, stubbed out a cigar and came outside.

"Hi, Rachel. I'm pleased I've run into you. Have you heard all that's been going on?"

"Let's grab a drink and you can tell me about it."

"Sure thing." Gaz looked as though he'd had too much sun again. His pale complexion resembled a beetroot.

"Do you like jazz?"

Gaz shrugged. "I don't mind it."

"Follow me," said Rachel, leading him to her favourite place, the Jazz Bar. Once they were settled in a booth, each with an Indian version of a well-known cocktail called a Tamarind Ginger Margarita, which was the special of the day, she waited for Gaz to give his take on events.

"Carol's been arrested," he blurted the words out, eyes popping.

"Really? Is this about Darrell?"

"Yeah. Stoney told us at tonight's meeting. She drugged Darrell and they reckon she killed him." He was shaking his head.

"You don't seem convinced."

"I'm not. You know you told me to think hard about that night; well, I've been doing just that. She drugged him – I'm not saying she didn't – but I don't think she needed to kill him, not after all the stirring she did with Stoney in the restaurant. I was sitting next to her, and every time Darrell did or said something odd, like, she and Sangie pointed it out. It wasn't hard to see he'd blown it by the time Stoney left, stone-faced and all." Gaz laughed at his own joke.

"What if she wanted to be certain?" Rachel argued, hoping he had more evidence than what he'd just shared.

He shook his head again. "Nah. She's not a killer. I've been talking to Matt, and he reckons he was with her most of the night, hoping to… well… you know. Anyway, he said she was pretty confident things were going her way on the job front. If anyone was going to stand in her way – according to Matt – it would be Lizzie. Did you hear it was Sangie who hit your friend?"

Rachel's lips tightened. "I did hear that, yes."

"Apparently, she was trying to get rid of the drugs, which turned out to be amphetamines, after Lizzie told her to be careful. Your friend happened to get in her way; the wrong place and all that. I don't understand why she did that, mind. She could have just run off. If anyone has it in them to kill Darrell, I reckon it's Sangie. Remember the car thing? That could have been her."

"It's a bit of a leap of the imagination to suggest because she hit out at someone while trying to dispose of drugs, she's also a killer. We can't be sure the car driver was aiming for Darrell, although it was odd at the time. They could have been a drunk."

Gaz stared sulkily into his glass, taking a drink through the straw before sucking at the lime added to the edge.

"I suppose, but Sangie is really ambitious. The Earl Spence thing is becoming much more obvious. They're off for secret rendezvous all the time. I followed them this afternoon."

"Wow!" said Rachel. "Isn't that a bit over the top?"

He giggled. "Maybe, but I was annoyed about security arresting Carol. Rosemary let me visit her, by the way. She admitted drugging Darrell, but she reckons Sangie might have thrown a rock at her yesterday afternoon. Before you saved her."

"What makes her think it was Sangita?"

"Dunno. I suppose she's annoyed about Sangie giving her a ring that made it look as though she hit your friend. She says if she'd drowned, they would've used it as evidence to suggest it was her that was violent, and conclude she'd also killed Darrell."

"I see," said Rachel, who had been thinking along similar lines herself. "What's the word on the street – or rather, within your group – about who's going to get the promotion?"

"To be honest, Lizzie and Matt are trying to fight it out between them while Lizzie pretends to be on both sides at the same time."

"Hedging her bets," suggested Rachel.

"Exactly. Sangie might be rich – or her dad might be – but she's not got the experience."

"Is that what you've heard or what you think?"

"Stoney's not giving much away. She's gone very quiet, actually. Lizzie thinks she might get the chop or be forced to resign. I'm not sure if that would help or hinder Earl."

"I can't see how it would help him. He wouldn't be in the running for CEO, surely?" Rachel asked.

"Definitely not, but with a new CEO, he might have even more influence. Although, if you ask me, he's got enough already. That man's poison. He hated Darrell."

"Why was that?" Rachel hadn't been able to understand why Earl singled Darrell out for his venom.

"Jealousy, I think." Gaz's mouth dropped open. "Hey, you don't think Earl could have killed him, do you?"

"It would have to be a weird jealousy. Darrell wasn't a threat to him."

"True. But he hates not getting his own way."

"Many people hate that," said Rachel. "But they don't commit murder. Besides, you have to admit, it's Carol under arrest for drugging Darrell, not Earl; or Sangita, for that matter."

Gaz dropped his head. "I just don't think Carol did it. I don't particularly like her, but after yesterday… you know? She's had a hard time."

"You were telling me about following Earl and Sangita. Where did they go?"

Gaz laughed. "I thought I'd catch them at it, but they went to the Observation Lounge on the top deck and chatted to a couple of Indian guys. I got bored waiting to see what they did next, so I left. They most likely rumbled me. I tried following them tonight after the meeting; they leave separately and meet up afterwards. I've clocked them doing that a couple of times, so I thought I'd see whose room they went to, just to tell the others we're right about the affair."

"And?"

Gaz sighed. "They went to the internet café and huddled round a computer."

"I see. Thanks for the drink, I'd better go."

Rachel left a gawping Gaz with an idea buzzing around in her head.

Chapter 29

Sarah got back to her room only to find the tall figure of Sangita Regum outside, dressed in a long, flowing turquoise evening dress. The younger woman tapped her foot impatiently as if it had been a drag having to wait.

Seeing her there with no indication of remorse caused a throbbing in Sarah's wrist. "How did you know where my room was?" she found herself snapping at the condescending woman with the false eyelashes and acrylic nails.

"Well, someone must have told me, or I wouldn't be here. Ah yes, that chief of security. What's his name again? Jack?"

"Chief Waverley. Don't let him hear you using his first name or he might change his mind about allowing you to stay." *I doubt she got the information from Waverley*, thought Sarah, guarded.

"He couldn't do anything about it, even if he wanted to."

"What do you want?"

"I was told to come and see you. And here I am." Sangita grinned until her shiny whites revealed a splash of lipstick on a rear molar. Hardly the picture of the penitent sinner, Sangita Regum looked every inch the schoolgirl bully.

"And?"

"Aren't you going to invite me inside? I'm not used to standing in corridors like a servant," said Sangita.

Sarah could believe that, but she didn't want this woman inside her and Jason's suite. She was torn between a desire to be rude and another to get this false apology over with.

Sarah opened the door and walked in. Sangita followed.

"My husband will be back any minute, so if you could be brief," Sarah said once they were inside.

Sangita appraised the living quarters with narrowing eyes. "Is this where you live? My servants have bigger rooms."

"I thought you had something you wanted to say to me," said Sarah.

"Oh, that." Sangita waved a dismissive hand. "How's the face, by the way? And that wrist… it must have hurt."

Sarah glared at the flintlike eyes staring at her. Instead of Sarah relishing the still missing apology, it was Sangita who was enjoying the exchange. Too much.

"Why don't you just get to the reason for your being here and we can both move on?"

"Not very friendly, are you? For a nurse, I mean. I would have thought you'd have to have some people skills for your job. Mind you, I bet they can't be too choosy on these mass-product cruise lines."

Sarah resisted taking the barb to heart and replied, "I'm also human, and as we usually have a zero tolerance policy to passengers attacking crew, I'd like you to get to the point of why you're in my living quarters." This woman was infuriating. Sarah could have kicked herself for admitting her into her safe haven.

"Living quarters… not your home, then? I suppose you don't have a home, having chosen the life of a nomad. Anyway, I told you already why I'm here."

"You said security instructed you to come and see me. At the request of your father, I understand?"

For a moment, Sangita appeared thrown, then her upper lip curled. "If you already know, why don't you say so? We could have got this over with by now."

Sarah folded her arms, waiting. "Please do."

Sangita gave the room another disparaging look. "Do you enjoy living here? I mean, it must be like living in a hutch. There's nowhere to put anything."

Sarah was pleased Sangita Regum hadn't seen her previous balcony suite, or any of the crew quarters below the waterline for that matter.

"It suits us fine."

"Fancy two of you squeezing in here. I'd find it claustrophobic myself. I don't think I could stand it. Even the so-called luxury apartments upstairs could do with more space. You don't need to look so hoity-toity; you know I'm right."

"If the suites aren't good enough for you, you can always leave when we arrive in Kochi tomorrow."

Sangita examined her fingernails, then moved over to Sarah's mirror, scrutinising her reflection. She had the audacity to remove lipstick from her purse and apply it, leaving Sarah open-mouthed.

"I might just do that if—"

"If what?" Sarah asked.

"Oh, nothing that concerns a lowly nurse. Anyway, this luxury cruise liner is nothing compared to my father's yacht." If her nostrils could have got any higher to show her distaste, Sangita would have been looking down from the ceiling.

Sarah bit her bottom lip to prevent herself from telling the woman what she could do with her opinions and her father's yacht.

"Look, it's been a long day and I'm tired. Can we just get this over with?"

"If you put it like that, why not?"

Something in the woman's malicious tone set alarm bells ringing in Sarah's head. Should she call for help? Sangita turned, positioning herself between Sarah and the door. Her wrist ached beneath the plaster, which was too light to be used as a weapon. Would she need a weapon?

She had already suffered enough pain at the hands of this dreadful woman.

Sarah felt lightheaded all of a sudden. She reached out for the bed, sitting down, and everything went black.

Chapter 30

Jason could have done without an extra night shift, but the brig needed covering. Someone had to check every hour so that Carol North didn't do anything stupid, and Rosemary had already covered for him the night Sarah was attacked.

"Is there a problem, Goodridge?" Waverley asked.

"No, sir. I'll telephone Sarah and let her know I won't be back tonight." He picked up the phone and dialled their room. The answer machine kicked in. "Hi, Sarah. Sorry, darling; Rosemary needs the night off, so I'm paying her back the shift I owe her. I'll bring you breakfast in the morning to make up for it. Love you."

"You could radio her if you think she'll be upset," Waverley offered.

"I can't. Her radio's been switched off since the attack. Gwen suggested it. It'll be fine. She's having dinner with Rachel, so she'll have lost track of time anyway."

Waverley nodded. "Before you go, your friend Rosa sent us an encrypted file. I assume it's more CCTV. She said to call her, and she'll let you know how to access it. At least that will keep your mind occupied while you're on sentry duty."

"Brilliant. Thank you, sir."

Jason left with a spring in his step, feeling much happier about pulling the night duty. There was nothing he liked more than peace and quiet to study evidence. First, he'd have a good catchup with Rosa because they hadn't been able to talk properly whenever he'd contacted her. There was always someone else around either his or her end.

The door to the office, which doubled as an interview room serving the brig, was open. Rosemary smiled.

"Sorry about this, Jason. If I'd known the boss would give you the shift, I would have cancelled."

"Are you going somewhere?" he asked.

"I've got a date."

"You kept that under your belt," said Jason, grinning. Ever since Rosemary had joined the ship, he'd only known her to visit the gym. "Someone from the fitness centre?"

A hint of a blush appeared on Rosemary's cheeks. "Maybe. Anyway, it's just a drink. We'll see what happens. Are you sure you don't want me to cancel?"

"And give you an excuse to back out? No way!"

"Actually I'm looking forward to it. All's quiet with Carol. Gary Jacobs visited earlier."

"Did you let him in there?" Jason frowned.

"No, I let him see her in here. Don't worry; I was outside the whole time and I don't believe he handed her a nail file."

Jason laughed. "Do I need to check on her now?"

"Just done it. You've got an hour to yourself. What are you going to do?"

"Watch some TV." Jason laughed.

"Right then, I'll see you sometime tomorrow. I guess she'll be gone by the time I come on shift." Rosemary inclined her head towards the occupied brig further down the corridor. "It's a shame."

"We just do as we're told," said Jason. "Enjoy your date."

"Thanks." Rosemary flushed again.

Jason wondered how long this had been going on. Rosemary was always friendly but hard to read. She liked her privacy. He sighed, wondering whether to call Sarah again. She might have gone to bed by now.

After calling down to the kitchen for a bottle of water and a pot of tea, he waited for the delivery before picking up the phone and dialling Rosa's number.

"You got the message, then?" Rosa picked up straight away.

"Not long ago. What is it?"

"I tracked down the one working camera from the alleyway where your vic was found. The police didn't find it because it's well hidden."

"Why?"

"Let's just say the proprietor's business isn't entirely legal. I had to use my powers of persuasion to get footage of the night in question."

"You threatened him, then," Jason said, smirking. Rosa's thunderous chortle hit his left ear, and he adjusted the phone.

"You know my motto. You gotta do what you gotta do."

"I hope you left him in one piece."

"How do you know it was a him? You're right, though, it was. To be fair, he was soft and flabby, and took little persuasion."

"Any idea what's on it?"

"Sorry, no. There was no time to look. We're flying up to New Delhi first thing, and have a few other things to check out before we leave. I don't like to leave anything to chance."

Jason remembered how Rosa was obsessive about checking her equipment ten times before going on any mission. She was also the fastest in their squadron at cleaning and reloading the SA80 IW. Rosa was OCD even before the sergeants drilled it into her. Ex-squaddies went one way or another: obsessive or chaotic. Rosa would always be the former.

"So how do I get in?"

"Just open the email and put my name in."

"The chief told me the file was encrypted."

"That was just so he'd keep his nose out. Besides, I enjoy hearing your sexy voice," she chortled again.

"Next time I'm in Mumbai, if you're there, I'll buy you a drink," Jason said, already opening the video files. Twelve hours' worth! "I'd love to have a proper catchup, but you sound busy." He could hear noise in the background.

"Yes, sorry, Jason; I gotta go. Give my regards to that wife of yours; she's a lucky woman."

"I will. Cheers, Rosa."

Jason sat back in his chair for a few minutes, remembering the good times they'd had. It wasn't often he got to recall happy memories from his time in Afghanistan, but Rosa was one of them.

He let the videos load while he went to check on Carol North. Peering through the window, he saw her sitting up, staring back at him. He opened the door.

"Am I free to go yet?"

"Sorry. Why don't you get some sleep?"

"As if... I've never been locked away before and I hate confined spaces." She brushed a tear from one eye. "You've got this all wrong, you know that?"

"I'm just about to find out whether that's the case."

She sat bolt upright. "How?"

"I've got fresh evidence to look at, so if you're really innocent, you'll want me to get on with it."

Hope filled her eyes as she waved him away. "Go. Yes, get on with it."

Jason hoped this video would give him answers because that wasn't the reaction of a guilty woman.

Chapter 31

Rachel tried to call Waverley, but there was no reply. He'd most likely gone to bed. She tried the medical centre and was pleased when Bernard answered.

"Hello, Rachel. What can I do for you at this ungodly hour? Your friend is still off sick."

"I know it goes against all the rules, but I need a favour."

Bernard's voice sounded guarded. "Which means you're about to do something the chief of security wouldn't approve of." He sniggered nervously.

"Not quite. I've tried to get hold of him, but I think he's off duty. He's been going on about how he needs to get early nights, so I don't want to disturb him."

"I know the feeling," said Bernard. "Tonight's been horrendous so far and it's still young for me. Shoot... what is it you want?"

Rachel told Bernard what she was after, and he was happy to oblige. She thanked him and hung up. After changing into jeans and a light jumper, Rachel headed upstairs to the VIP suite, muttering to herself. Her brain wasn't functioning on all cylinders, that's for sure. Sarah had mentioned on the first day where the Rejuvenescence Pharma party was staying, but she'd forgotten. The number written on the note in her hand was the same suite Lord and Lady Fanston had stayed in on her previous cruise.

And you know how that ended, her inner nemesis whispered.

Once outside the area that was sealed off from other guests, Rachel hid behind a post, waiting for someone who wouldn't recognise her to open the secure door. It was dark and getting late, so her efforts might prove fruitless if no-one came. Still, once her mind was set on something, there was no going back.

It was shortly after eleven when a member of the crew headed inside. Rachel tailgated the woman, grabbing hold of the door.

"Good evening," she said with a smile, hoping not to be challenged.

"Hello, ma'am." As the woman scurried along the corridor and out to the private pool area where she set about collecting used glasses from tables, Rachel stood outside Tia Stone's door. Now she was here, she hesitated. What if Dr Stone was asleep? Her visit might not be well received.

Taking a deep breath, she steeled herself, readying for an onslaught, and knocked. The door opened almost immediately and a red-eyed Dr Stone frowned.

"What are you doing here?"

"I know this is going to seem crazy, me turning up like this, but I really need to talk to you if we're going to catch the person who killed Darrell."

Tia didn't move, weighing up what Rachel had said. Eventually, she asked, "Do you work for the cruise line?"

"Not exactly," Rachel answered honestly, "but I've lent a hand in the past. Back in the UK, I'm a detective. My name's Rachel."

"Yes, we met in Dr Bentley's office." Appearing satisfied, Tia Stone stepped aside, allowing Rachel inside. The first thing she noticed was steam coming from a cup of black coffee on the table.

"I've not been sleeping well," Tia explained, appearing more vulnerable without the business suit and makeup. "I take it you don't believe Carol killed Darrell or you wouldn't be here."

"Correct. She was silly, but she doesn't strike me as a murderer. Besides, I think someone tried to kill her in Goa."

"The swimming accident? Perhaps you'd better tell me what you think I can help you with, but I must warn you, I don't know what's going on. My company seems to have catapulted out of control, from success to liability within days." She threw her hands up in the air before collapsing back onto the plush sofa.

Rachel sat opposite. "First tell me why you changed your mind about Darrell getting the promotion and turned this trip into a competition."

Tia's eyes hardened. "Who are you to challenge my business decisions?"

"Bear with me," said Rachel. "I believe it's significant."

Tia reached for her mug, cupping both hands around it. "There's a coffee machine over there if you want to help yourself," she said.

Rachel did as bid before returning to her position, waiting patiently for Tia to open up.

"You seem well briefed. I won't ask how you've come to be so because it makes little difference now. You're right. I was going to give Darrell the promotion; he has… rather, had proved himself capable and would have made a good right-hand man. As we'd recently floated on the stock exchange in the US, it made sense to have someone out there I could trust.

"Unfortunately, the senior scientists haven't been getting along, too busy vying for position. His promotion would have put a stop to that eventually, but I needed their cooperation now. There's always a competitive element in big business, but before the behaviour got out of control, I organised the team-building holiday. I thought if they all got together and relaxed, they might pull together."

"Why did you invite Gary Jacobs along when he's not a senior research scientist?"

"You're well informed, Rachel. Any other time I'd be annoyed. I invited Gary because he works with me in the

Dublin office. He's highly intelligent when he applies himself, so I thought I'd give him the opportunity to mingle with the others with a view to taking Darrell's place."

"But something changed," said Rachel.

"At the last board meeting before the start of this holiday, the directors expressed doubt and felt I was being too hasty in putting Darrell in charge. There was even a suggestion I was being soft. I don't know where it came from, but someone had sowed doubt about my leadership. I listened when they suggested Earl and I should join the scientists on the trip. I agreed we would assess together who was the best candidate for the job."

"Did you not have the power to tell them it was your decision?" Rachel asked.

"In retrospect, that's what I should have done." Tia stared into space. "The company has since been badly damaged. Information is being leaked all over the place. I've decided to sell."

Realisation dawned on Rachel as she mulled this statement over.

"Decided to, or been forced to?"

"What does it matter? The decision's made."

"It matters a great deal if you know who's behind the leaks."

Tia pursed her lips. "I don't. I thought I could ride it out, but after a lengthy board meeting today, the directors outvoted me. We're selling. Everything I've worked for.

Everything I've built up… is now going to someone else who will profit from it."

"Who's buying?"

"It's a conglomerate called Mycil Holdings. They jumped on the poor publicity and set up a hostile takeover. The board panicked… don't feel sorry for me. I'll walk away from it quite rich, but that isn't the point. It was never about the money for me; it was all about creating something that would benefit humanity."

Rachel did feel sorry for Tia Stone. "What if someone has been deliberately reporting you to the board, undermining you, your methods and your management with a view to forcing this takeover?"

Tia shook her head. "I can't believe that. I've grown this company from scratch, putting together the best in the business. People have invested time and money. It's impossible. Who would want to do such a thing?"

"I've got an idea, but I need your help to expose them. I believe it's someone with contacts in high places. We have got little time."

Rachel explained what she wanted Tia to do and what she hoped to gain from it. Tia listened carefully and seemed convinced enough that Rachel was on the right track. If she was, the killer would come after her.

"Why would you put yourself in danger like this?" said Tia. "I'm not sure I should allow it."

"I won't be alone. I'll brief the chief of security first thing in the morning and wear a wire."

"In that case, I will do as you suggest, but please be careful. If what you say is true, you'll be in grave danger."

"And so will you be, unless you execute the plan exactly as I've said. Don't let on you know anything. Just make out I'm an interfering busybody and you've sent me away with a piece of your mind."

"I can do that."

Rachel left Tia believing her plan would work. She just had to wait until morning, persuade Waverley to go along with it and get the wire. Nothing would go wrong. It's not like she hadn't done this kind of thing before.

Chapter 32

On the way out of the VIP annexe, Rachel ducked behind a pillar when she saw Gaz, Matt and Lizzie wobbling towards the entrance. Now wasn't the time for a chat. No-one must know what Tia was doing. She waited while Matt smoked a cigarette.

"It's a shame Darrell isn't here to enjoy this," Gaz was speaking.

"What?" Lizzie asked.

"Us getting on and all. If this had just been a team-building exercise like it was meant to be, I reckon it would have worked."

"Except he'd have got the promotion," Lizzie sneered.

"You think you're going to get it, don't you?" Matt said. They were obviously unaware the company was about to be sold.

"I'm the best qualified now Carol's out of the running."

"What about Pantoni?" Gaz challenged.

"Give me a break. She doesn't stand a chance."

If Rachel didn't already have a suspect, Lizzie Meeton might be climbing the list. She could be involved, though. Best not to rule anything out, just in case her theory was wrong or incomplete.

"And what makes you think you do?" Matt challenged. "I've got just as much chance as you have."

"Except you're in Wales. Hardly the business centre of the world." Lizzie let her words hang in the air before adding, "Where is Pantoni anyway?"

"I expect she's off sulking somewhere. Has anyone seen Sangie?" Gaz asked.

"Nope. And I don't want to either," said Matt. "She'll be with Spence somewhere. That girl's too much up her own backside, if you ask me."

Rachel had to stop herself laughing at the description of the jumped-up Sangita Regum.

"I'm gonna call it a night," Matt said. "I'm looking forward to getting off this ship for a while."

"Watch you don't have another asthma attack when you do," Lizzie shouted after him as he made his way through the annexe door.

"That was nasty. Why do you do it when we were getting on?" Gaz asked after Matt had left.

"I'm not sure. I just speak as I find. He's been moaning about his damn breathing for days."

"You can't blame him for that. He has to carry his inhaler everywhere."

"So why get off the ship at all? The pollution's much worse on land."

"Because he gets seasick," said Gaz.

Rachel could almost imagine Lizzie's eye roll as she sneered, "Oh, spare me from wimps. Anyway, I'm going to my bed. Are you coming?"

"I'd be delighted," said Gaz.

Lizzie chuckled. "In your dreams. I meant, are you coming inside?"

"I know what you meant." Gaz laughed. "You're not my type anyway."

Rachel heard them bantering until the door closed. She must have been hiding out there for about twenty minutes. Rachel shivered, wishing she'd worn a jacket.

When she got back inside the public area of the ship, her phone buzzed in her handbag. It was a message from Sarah.

"I've discovered something important. Jason's working tonight. Come to my room."

Rachel's body longed for sleep. She wondered if a telephone call would do, but Sarah's news might be *really* important and she didn't want her friend doing anything dangerous. With a long sigh, she headed down a few floors to Sarah's room.

The door was jammed open with a book. She picked the book up and walked in.

"You really shouldn't—" Her mouth dropped along with her heart.

"You look surprised." Earl Spence was standing behind Sarah, whose hands were bound, holding a knife to her throat.

"You?" Rachel could have kicked herself. All the evidence had pointed to Sangita, but now the last link clicked into place. Or were they in it together? Rachel looked into Sarah's wide eyes and tried to nod reassuringly.

"Ah, I see now," said Earl. "You thought it was Sangita."

"Is she involved, or just a pawn in your deadly game?" The door had closed behind her – blasted security doors – but Rachel remained in the narrow hallway leading into Sarah and Jason's lounge. If she kept him talking, perhaps she would get a chance to surprise him.

"Sangita has been a go-between for me, yes. Her father is going to buy out the company and I'll get an enormous fee for my part in it. I might even be CEO."

"I hardly think you're qualified," said Rachel.

"The only qualification in Muhmad Regum's book is loyalty."

"What would you know about loyalty?" Rachel knew she risked riling him but couldn't help herself. His hand actually loosened on Sarah as he waved the knife at Rachel.

"More than you think. Who are you anyway? You don't even work on board this ship."

Rachel grimaced. "I'm someone who just happens to be in your way."

"I don't suppose you'd be interested in a deal?" he asked. "You're obviously resourceful as well as beautiful."

"I don't do deals with murderers," she said. "Men like you sicken me."

Spence grabbed Sarah again. "I suggest, if you want to leave this room alive, you treat me with a little more respect."

Rachel held her palms up. "Okay, fine. You win. Don't hurt her."

"That's more like it. Now, I'm exiting this ship in the morning. All I need you and your friend to do is have a little sleep. Before that, though, I want you to put those on."

Rachel followed Earl's eyes to a pair of handcuffs on the bed.

"Don't do it, Rachel," called Sarah. "Run!"

Rachel considered her options.

"I wouldn't try if I were you. I'm very good with this knife and I could have an excellent shot at you before you even got to the door. If I have to do that, I will unfortunately need to kill your friend as well."

"How can I trust you to let us go?"

"I have nothing against you. Muhmad's a powerful man who has members of the Mumbai police in his pocket. I just need to get to get to Mumbai. You can't harm me once I'm ashore, believe me. The sale will still go through. Stone's finished."

"Does Mr Regum know you kill people?"

"He knows I get things done. I don't think he cares how that happens. Men like him don't get to where they are without breaking a few laws."

"I wonder if he'll consider murder a law he's willing to break."

"If you want the truth, I did not mean Baker to die. He was meant to be incapacitated. The idiot was so drunk he flopped like a sack."

Rachel remembered the car. "Did you also hire the car driver who nearly killed him?"

"I only hired him to scare him, that's all."

"What about Sangita? Does she know you killed Darrell? You can't say you didn't try to kill Carol."

"Sangita thinks Carol killed Baker and that her mishap in the sea was an accident. Tia wasn't getting the message; she was going to promote Carol."

"Why did Sangita give Carol the ring?"

"What ring? Oh, that. I don't know; she wouldn't have done if she had known it would be used in evidence. But as I mentioned earlier, her father can keep her out of trouble. I just needed her to arrange meetings."

Earl was relaxing, showing off almost. He wanted to show how clever he was, didn't see Rachel as a threat. Always a dangerous mistake.

"I must admit, I'm impressed. You've been working behind the scenes, contacting the board to undermine Dr Stone as well as causing friction within the team. How long has this been in the planning?"

Earl smirked. "Six months." His face darkened. "Ever since I found out my wife was having an affair with Tia Stone's brother. Can you believe it?" Venom filled his face and eyes. "The worst of it is, I introduced them; invited

Tia and her brother to stay in our home. And this is how she repays me."

Rachel didn't want him angry. "These things are rarely planned. I'm sure neither of them meant to hurt you." Why he was blaming Tia rather than her brother or his wife, Rachel couldn't see.

"I didn't work it out at first. My wife told me she wanted a divorce. I guessed she was seeing someone else; I just needed to find out who, see if I could buy them off. I hired a private investigator."

Rachel thought of Carlos. He hated doing matrimonial acrimony jobs. For a brief second, she wondered if any of the women or men he had discovered having affairs had come to harm. But not everyone was a psychopath.

"So instead of trying to buy Dr Stone's brother off, you hatched an ingenious plan to remove the world from under her feet. How does that harm her brother?"

"My wife was going to take everything and share it with that idiot. I've worked my fingers to the bone to give her the world. She's younger than me, don't you know? Tia should never have brought him into my home and forced him on my wife. I'm going to start a new life by myself. I'll be able to afford to have any woman I want."

"Isn't this whole warped charade more about money than revenge?"

"It's about both, Rachel." The ice-cold eyes convinced Rachel that unless she did something soon, neither she nor Sarah would leave this room alive. It would be hard to stall him for much longer.

She moved slowly towards the bed and picked up the handcuffs as if she was about to comply with his command. Once they were in her hands, she played with them.

"But Tia's brother and your wife still continue their relationship, even after all of this. What have you gained other than money?"

Spence moved the knife away from Sarah's neck once more. Pointing it at Rachel, he gritted his teeth.

"I'll ruin both Stones. You've heard the saying; I won't leave a Stone unturned." An evil cackle filled the room. "This is just the beginning."

"What about your wife?" Rachel asked.

"She's the mother of my children. I won't harm her."

Rachel gave Sarah a quick nod before lunging at Spence, who had dropped his guard enough to give her space.

"Run, Sarah," she cried.

Rachel swung the handcuffs at his face, taking him by surprise. She rounded on Spence while he put one hand to his face. He was stronger than he looked, but Rachel had hold of the knife hand while she brought her knee up to his groin. He bent over double, dropping the weapon. Rachel used double-gripped hands to hit him between the shoulder blades, then she dug her knee into the small of his back, forcing him to the floor. It didn't take long to pull his hands behind his back and put them in the handcuffs he had intended for her.

She pushed him away, disgusted.

Sarah was still at the door.

"What part of run didn't you understand?" Rachel grinned, breathing hard. Sarah ran over to her and Rachel removed the rope from her wrists, taking care not to hurt her injured arm any more than the despicable Earl Spence had already done and pulling her into a hug. "Time to call your husband."

The door burst open and Jason, Waverley, and security officer Ravanos ran in, staring at the scene. Jason rushed over and held his wife while Waverley and Ravanos pulled Earl Spence to his feet.

"These women kidnapped me, don't you see?" he yelled.

"And I'm an alien," said Waverley. He turned round and looked at Rachel. "Are you okay?"

"I'm good, thanks."

"We can go through what happened in the morning. Goodridge, you have the rest of the night off. I'll release Miss North and look after this one myself."

"Yes, sir," said Jason, still holding Sarah. He mouthed a thank you to Rachel, who had a mountain of questions but decided they would have to wait until morning. Sarah had suffered enough for one night.

"I'll say goodnight, then," said Waverley grinning at Rachel. "Come on. Let's get this man down to the brig."

Ravanos and Waverley steered Earl Spence through the door which closed behind them.

"Thank you, Rachel. I didn't send that text; I wouldn't." Sarah looked down at her feet. "I grabbed the phone when he came into the room meaning to call for help, but he took it from me once I'd unlocked it."

"I'm glad he did message me," Rachel said. "Now, it's time for you to get some rest. We'll speak tomorrow."

She went back to her room, hardly daring to contemplate the idea that if Earl hadn't tried to be quite so clever, he could have killed Sarah, and then come after her. She shuddered.

Chapter 33

Gwen's office was packed by the time Rachel arrived. As soon as she walked in, a round of applause rang out. She felt herself blush, waiting for them to stop. The sea of friendly faces stood out in stark contrast to Earl Spence's evil sneer the night before.

"Right then, you lot. You've got surgery to go to," Gwen ordered. Bernard slapped Rachel on the back, grinning as he left the room. Brigitte gave her a smile.

"Thank you for rescuing Sarah. I don't know what I'd do without her." A tear threatened to spill down the French nurse's face, but she quickly brushed it away.

Janet Plover leaned in and whispered, "Nice one, Rachel. Now, please can you enjoy your holiday?"

Rachel laughed. Dr Bentley was the only one missing. She assumed he was busy doing room visits.

"Coffee?" Gwen offered, already moving towards the machine that provided the team with an everlasting supply, except for when their steward brought in fresh pots of tea and coffee from the kitchens.

"Yes, please." Rachel joined Sarah on the sofa while Waverley paced the floor, coughing impatiently. Jason was sitting on a chair with tea in hand.

"Would you like some of my fruit tea, chief?" Gwen asked.

"I didn't know you had any. Yes, that would be very nice, thank you."

Rachel suspected Gwen had requested a supply especially.

"Then, for goodness' sake, sit down before you wear a hole in the carpet," the senior nurse ordered.

Waverley obeyed.

Once they were all seated with drinks in front of them, Rachel and Waverley started speaking at the same time.

"Sorry. You first," said the chief.

"I wanted to know how Earl Spence came to be in Sarah's room and how you…" she looked from Waverley to Jason "… knew where to come."

Sarah answered. "I had a strange visit from Sangita Regum first. She was being a right pain and became threatening. I'm afraid I was rather pathetic and fainted. Thankfully, I sat on the bed first. I woke with her sponging me down, offering me a glass of water. She was quite nice after that – I guess she knew she was on a final warning. Anyway, she stayed for some time, making sure I was fully recovered before offering the briefest of apologies and leaving.

"I was still recovering from the visit and the faint when I heard a knock at the door. I didn't use the spyhole, assuming Sangita had forgotten something." Sarah cast a regretful look Jason's way. "As soon as I opened it, Earl Spence barged in, manhandling me back into the room. He shoved me into the chair. I reached for my phone, and I think he deliberately waited for me to unlock it before snatching it away again. He disabled the lock screen – I keep the code in my notes along with passwords – and then tied my hands. My poor wrist! I yelled at him, telling him he would be in big trouble when my husband, who's a security guard, got back at any minute. That was the only time he looked less than confident.

"It was then I noticed the answerphone flashing. He must have followed my eyes because he strolled over to the machine and pressed the button. That's when we both realised Jason wouldn't be coming back. To be honest, I think if he hadn't heard that message, I'd have been dropped over the side."

Sarah's bottom lip trembled. They waited for her to gather herself together, all taking a sip of whatever they were drinking. Apart from Jason, who put a reassuring hand on his wife's shoulder.

"It's fine. Just the aftershock," she said. "He taunted me about the message, and then tapped into my phone. I asked what he was doing, and he just told me, 'You'll see'. The next thing, he put a book down on the floor to wedge the door open before standing behind me and removing a flick knife from his pocket."

"How the hell did he get that on board my ship?" It was Waverley's first interruption and Rachel doubted it would be the last.

"My guess would be Sangita," said Rachel. "Foolish girl wouldn't know what he wanted it for. In fact, it was probably initially a souvenir."

"Anyway, that's when Rachel came in," said Sarah. "Although I was terrified he was going to kill both of us, somehow I knew Rachel could get the better of him. The more you kept him talking, Rachel, the more his grip on me relaxed. When you walked over to the bed and picked up the handcuffs, I readied myself. I knew if you put those cuffs on, we were both dead."

Rachel touched Sarah's hand. "Thank you for trusting me."

Jason's eyes were filling up. "Thank *you*," he managed.

"But how did you know where we were?" Rachel asked Waverley.

"Ah, that's the other part of the story. Tell them, Goodridge."

"Some of you know I have a contact in Mumbai. Yesterday, she acquired some footage from dubious premises in the alleyway where Darrell Baker's body was discovered. It took me a while to trawl through it, as the timestamp wasn't working. There was a lot of nothing to view before I saw Baker. He was agitated, kept staring at his watch. I don't think he could register what time it was. He seemed totally out of it.

"Finally, someone else came into view. At first, I could only see the back of the person sneaking up from behind while Baker was relieving himself against a shop's façade."

"Disgusting," said Gwen.

"Baker had refastened his trousers when he was struck from behind. He fell heavily into a pile of boxes. That's when Earl Spence looked up. He must have heard something at the top of the alley because he pretended to be making a phone call. At least, that's what I think he was doing. Once he seemed satisfied the distraction had gone, he rained down another blow onto the helpless fellow before casually strolling away."

"So much for him not meaning to kill Darrell," said Rachel.

"Is that what he said?" Waverley asked.

"Yep."

"He meant to kill him all right," said Jason. "The first blow would have done him enough damage and might have proved fatal on its own. The second was insurance."

"That still doesn't explain how you knew where he was," said Rachel.

"Once I had the evidence, I called the chief. We found Spence's room empty. Dr Stone heard the kerfuffle and came out to see what was going on. When we told her, she said Rachel had asked her to let Spence know she had been asking questions. She said Rachel suspected Sangita of planning a takeover with her father, using Earl as the go-between. Good call, by the way." Jason looked at Rachel.

"Not really. I was convinced it was Sangita, in league with her father, who was pulling the strings. I had concluded that Earl was involved in that side of things but didn't think he'd resort to murder."

"That's because we didn't know his other motive," said Sarah.

Rachel explained to the confused trio about his wife's affair. "He wanted to destroy everything Tia Stone had worked for. But go on. How did you find us?"

"At first we checked your room, Rachel, and couldn't find you," said Jason. "We went back to the VIP suite and dragged them all out of bed, making it clear what would happen if any harm had come to you—"

"We didn't know at the time that Sarah was in danger," Waverley interrupted.

"We interviewed Sangita separately and told her about the footage. She seemed genuinely shocked. Spence must have killed Darrell when he was outside for *a breath of air*. Sangita admitted to plotting with her father and Earl to take over the company, but she had no idea about the rest. That's when she told us Earl had asked for Sarah's suite number. He'd told her he was going to have flowers sent on her behalf to smooth things over. The rest you know. We called Ravanos and prayed we weren't too late." Jason ran a hand through Sarah's hair.

"But as always," Waverley sighed, "you got there before us." He gave Rachel a sly grin. "You'll need to tell us everything the man told you so we can put it to him when we interview him. Then we'll hand him and the statement over to the Mumbai police. He'll be taken into custody in Kochi when we dock."

"But he told us Muhmad Regum has the Mumbai police in his pocket," said Rachel.

"That may well be," Waverley looked smug, "but his daughter has called him to inform him of one murder and one attempted murder. Apparently, Mr Regum might skirt the law when it comes to business, but he doesn't condone murder. Whatever Spence thinks might happen, he's in for a surprise when he finds himself inside an Indian prison."

"Good. I hope he gets what he deserves," said Rachel. "As we'll be docking soon, I need to eat. I want to visit Vypin Island. There's a famous lighthouse I'd like to see."

"I'm pleased to see you can switch off so quickly," said Gwen.

"It's just another case," said Rachel, winking at Sarah. "Are you joining me today?"

Sarah looked at Jason.

"It'll do you good. Hopefully, you can keep Rachel out of mischief and she can keep you safe."

"Well, if that's all, I'm going to grab brunch," Rachel said.

"Just one more thing," said Waverley. "What made those marks on Spence's face?"

"Jason's handcuffs," said Rachel, laughing. "They make a great weapon."

Rachel could still hear the guffaws as she left the medical centre, followed by happy chatter. Her legs were still trembling when she got to the buffet. It wasn't as easy to shake things off these days. She sat by a window watching the ship dock. How long before PTSD got so bad she could no longer work?

Chapter 34

Rachel and Sarah spent the afternoon visiting historical sights. It turned out they wouldn't be in Kochi long enough to get to Vypin Island, and Rachel's legs were still suffering the aftereffects of the sea rescue, but there was still a lot to see in a short space of time.

The first stop was Fort Kochi, built on the harbour by the Portuguese. The British had occupied it during their rule of India and it had a mixture of architecture from various other occupations. After wandering around the area for an hour, they went on to Bolgatty Island to savour the breathtaking views of the bay before visiting the palace of the same name.

They returned to the bay and stopped for afternoon chai in a traditional Indian teahouse where they were served sweet tea with goat's milk. Rachel grimaced after a mouthful.

"Boy, this takes some getting used to. It's like drinking condensed milk."

Sarah threw her head back, happy and relaxed. "Get it down you. The sugar will do you good. You're wasting away."

Rachel patted her abdomen. "Hardly! I've consumed more food in the past five days than I have in months."

"That's my point. Oh look, here comes dessert."

"When did you order that?"

"While you were taking photos of the bay."

Rachel tutted when a platter of sweet delights was placed on the table.

"That's jalebi; trust me, it's delicious." Sarah pointed to a pile of swirly orange sweets. "And that's laddu."

"I'll try this one." Rachel picked up one of the sweet balls Sarah had told her was laddu. It tasted of nutty semolina.

"I forgot to tell you because I didn't want to bring up last night again," said Sarah, picking up a jalebi and putting it in her mouth. "Mmm, this is so delicious."

"You were saying?" Rachel watched while her friend came down from food heaven. She couldn't deny Sarah needed the treats.

"Tia's told the board what Earl Spence has done and how he had plotted with the Regums to force them to sell on the cheap. Sangita's resigned, by the way, with immediate effect, and left the ship this morning."

Rachel tried one of the jalebis Sarah had waxed lyrical about. It was crunchy and very sweet but fruity at the same time.

After finally getting it down, she said, "More like she jumped before being pushed."

"I expect you're right. Anyway, the board informed Tia that Earl has been feeding misinformation to them for months. He was going to each one in confidence and blaming her for the friction among their top scientists. It was he who persuaded them to insist on the trip so he could 'oversee'..." Sarah used air quotes "...what was going on. All the time, he was stirring up mischief and turning the scientists against each other. That way he fed into their ambitious plans, making each one of them think they were in line for the promotion while plotting with Sangita's father to foster a hostile takeover. It appears he contacted Muhmad Regum once the India office opened."

"He excluded Gaz from the plotting and stirring?"

"Yes. Spence left him out because he works in the Dublin offices and he didn't want Tia getting wind of it. Anyway, the good news is, Tia is back in the company's good books and can run it with complete freedom. Carol was released last night. I think Waverley felt she'd learned her lesson and decided not to report her to the authorities in India."

"Fair enough. She was stupid, but I think the near-drowning will have a lasting impact on her."

"That's what Waverley told Jason. It's not like him to be so lenient. Still, I think he made the right decision under the circumstances."

"So, who gets the promotion?" Rachel helped herself to another laddu, pushing the sweet tea away.

"Guess?"

Rachel chewed, savouring the new tastes. "You know, this really is good. I suppose Lizzie or Matt," she said.

"I love it when you're wrong. It's such a rarity. Tia has decided to go for the one she believes has the profile and experience to pull the team together: Pearl Pantoni."

Rachel smiled. "Good choice. Pearl's older and – although it's not always the case, as showed by Earl Spence – most probably wiser."

After finishing dessert, Sarah went to use the facilities. Rachel walked across the road and was looking out on the bay when her phone buzzed, bearing the news she had been dreaming of.

"Just landed in Rome. Some suspicions, but nothing conclusive. Will call you as soon as I come out of debrief." Joy flooded through her, and it must have been obvious because, as soon as Sarah returned, she stopped dead.

"You've heard from Carlos."

Rachel could only nod, tears of relief flooding down her cheeks.

THE END

Author's Note

Thank you for reading *Corporate Cruise Murder*, the eleventh book in my Rachel Prince Mystery series. If you have enjoyed it, please leave an honest review on Amazon and/or any other platform you may use. I love receiving feedback from readers.

Keep in touch:
Signup for my no-spam newsletter and receive a FREE novella. You will also receive news of new releases and special offers, and have the opportunity to enter competitions.
Join now:
https://www.dawnbrookespublishing.com
Follow me on Facebook:
https://www.facebook.com/dawnbrookespublishing/
Follow me on YouTube:
https://www.youtube.com/c/DawnBrookesPublishing

Books by Dawn Brookes

Rachel Prince Mysteries

A Cruise to Murder

Deadly Cruise

Killer Cruise

Dying to Cruise

A Christmas Cruise Murder

Murderous Cruise Habit

Honeymoon Cruise Murder

A Murder Mystery Cruise

Hazardous Cruise

Captain's Dinner Cruise Murder

Corporate Cruise Murder

Treacherous Cruise Flirtation (Coming soon 2023)

Lady Marjorie Snellthorpe Mysteries

Death of a Blogger (Prequel Novella)

Murder at the Opera House

Murder in the Highlands

Murder at the Christmas Market (Coming soon 2022)

Murder at a Wimbledon Mansion (Coming soon 2023)

Carlos Jacobi PI

Body in the Woods
The Bradgate Park Murders
The Museum Murders (Coming soon 2023)

Memoirs

Hurry up Nurse: memoirs of nurse training in the 1970s
Hurry up Nurse 2: London calling
Hurry up Nurse 3: More adventures in the life of a student nurse

Picture Books for Children

Acknowledgements

Thank you to my editor Alison Jack, as always, for her kind comments about the book and for suggestions, corrections and amendments that make it a more polished read.

Thanks to my beta readers for comments and suggestions, and for their time given to reading the early drafts, and to my ARC team – I couldn't do without you. **Thanks to my beta readers for comments and suggestions, and for their time given to reading the early drafts, and to my ARC team – I couldn't do without you.** And a big thank you to Alex Davis for the final proofread picking up those punctuation errors and annoying typos!

I'm hugely grateful to my immediate circle of family and friends, who remain patient while I'm absorbed in my fictional world. Thanks for your continued support in all my endeavours.

I have to say thank you to my cruise-loving friends for joining me on some of the most precious experiences of my life, and to all the cruise lines for making every holiday a special one.

About the Author

Award winning author, Dawn Brookes holds an MA in Creative Writing with Distinction and is author of the Rachel Prince Mystery series, combining a unique blend of murder, cruising and medicine with a touch of romance. A spinoff series with Lady Marjorie Snellthorpe taking the lead is in progress with the prequel novella *Death of a Blogger* available in eBook, paperback and as an audiobook.

She also writes crime fiction featuring a tenacious PI which may be of interest to fans of Rachel Jacobi-Prince.

Dawn has a 39-year nursing pedigree and takes regular cruise holidays, which she says are for research purposes! She brings these passions together with a Christian background and a love of clean crime to her writing.

The surname of Rachel Prince is in honour of her childhood dog, Prince, who used to put his head on her knee while she lost herself in books.

Dawn's bestselling memoirs outlining her nurse training are available to buy. *Hurry up Nurse: memoirs of nurse training in the 1970s, Hurry up Nurse 2: London calling,* and *Hurry up*

Nurse 3: More adventures in the life of a student nurse. Dawn worked as a hospital nurse, midwife, district nurse and community matron across her career. Before turning her hand to writing for a living, she had multiple articles published in professional journals and coedited a nursing textbook.

She grew up in Leicester, later moved to London and Berkshire, but now lives in Derby. Dawn holds a Bachelor's degree with Honours and a Master's degree in education. Writing across genres, she also writes for children. Dawn has a passion for nature and loves animals, especially dogs. Animals will continue to feature in her children's books, as she believes caring for animals and nature helps children to become kinder human beings.